Other Dover Books by R. T. Campbell

Swing Low, Swing Death

Death for Madame

Unholy Dying

BODIES IN A BOOKSHOP

R. T. Campbell

Foreword by
Peter Main

DOVER PUBLICATIONS, INC.
Mineola, New York

Bibliographical Note

This Dover edition, first published in 2018, is an unabridged and unaltered republication of the work originally published by John Westhouse (Publishers) Ltd., London, April 1946, under the title *Bodies in a Bookshop: A Detective Story*. R. T. Campbell is the pseudonym of Ruthven Todd. A new Foreword by Peter Main has been specially prepared for this volume.

Library of Congress Cataloging-in-Publication Data

Names: Todd, Ruthven, 1914–1978, author.
Title: Bodies in a bookshop / R. T. Campbell.
Description: Mineola, New York : Dover Publications, Inc., 2018. | Series: Dover mystery classics series
Identifiers: LCCN 2017039665 | ISBN 9780486784434 | ISBN 0486784436
Subjects: LCSH: Murder—Investigation—Fiction. | London (England)—Fiction. | Bookstores—Fiction. | Botanists—Fiction. | GSAFD: Mystery fiction.
Classification: LCC PR6039.O26 B6 2018 | DDC 823/.914—dc23
LC record available at https://lccn.loc.gov/2017039665

Manufactured in the United States by LSC Communications
78443602   2019
www.doverpublications.com

Contents

CONTENTS

Foreword

R. T. CAMPBELL was the pen name of Ruthven Campbell Todd, a man better known under his real name as a poet and leading authority on the printing techniques of William Blake. The true identity of R. T. Campbell was not revealed to the world until the publication of Julian Symons's 1972 history of crime fiction, *Bloody Murder* (published in the United States as *Mortal Consequences*). Symons was a close friend of Todd, who had agreed readily enough to be unmasked. Symons recorded that Todd had written ten detective stories under the name R. T. Campbell, published by John Westhouse, and that the novels were "now distinctly rare." In a revised edition after Todd's death, Symons had to change his tune somewhat: "ten" novels became "twelve."

"A pleasant uncertainty prevails about the publication of four among the twelve books. Did *The Hungry Worms Are Waiting* ever see print, or did Westhouse go broke first? No copy of it is known to have appeared in any specialized bookseller's list."

This uncertainty has since been resolved, and it is now known that only eight novels were published, although Todd probably wrote four more. The missing novels were repeatedly advertised by Westhouse as "forthcoming," but they never forthcame because in 1948 Westhouse went into liquidation.

Todd wrote the novels toward the end of World War II, when he was living in rural Essex, England, having been bombed out of his apartment in central London. He wrote them at speed and claimed he finished one of them in three days. Throughout his life, he remained dismissive of their quality, saying they were "hack work," which he wrote to make money he badly needed to support himself while engaged in what he regarded as his more serious work: poetry and art history. Although the novels are uneven in quality, it is difficult to read them without feeling that he rather enjoyed writing them. Westhouse paid him two hundred pounds for each manuscript—quite a considerable amount at the time!

He was advised by fellow poet Cecil Day Lewis, who wrote detective novels as Nicholas Blake, to try his hand at detective fiction as a means of making money, but to use a pen name in order to avoid "ruining his name." Thus, Todd gave birth to R. T. Campbell by reworking his own full name. These books were his only foray into crime fiction, with the exception of *Mister Death's Blue-Eyed Boy* (set in New York City's Greenwich Village), which was never published and which Todd later said the manuscript was "probably happily, now lost." He also wrote two short stories in crime magazines under his real name, which later found their way into anthologies published by Mystery Writers of America.

Todd's novels are comedic, and all but one of the published works (*Apollo Wore a Wig*, a spy caper in the style of John Buchan's *The Thirty-Nine Steps*) feature a botanist-cum-amateur detective, Professor John Stubbs. The blurb on the dust jacket of his debut appearance in *Unholy Dying* tells us Stubbs is "an explosive and fallible character in the long English tradition of engaging comic figures. Professor Stubbs sets out to unravel the crime with considerable energy and the tact of a herd of elephants."

Stubbs is corpulent, mustachioed, opinionated, smokes a pipe filled with evil-smelling tobacco, and constantly swills beer from a quart mug in order to overcome his susceptibility to "dehydration." He cheerfully accuses innocent people of murder and lumbers on, unabashed, to find the true culprit. His "Watson" for most of the books is Max Boyle, with whom he has an engagingly prickly relationship, as he does with his sparring partner Inspector Reginald Bishop of Scotland Yard.

Here are the seven published Stubbs novels and their publication dates in the order they were presumably written, based on references that appear within them to previously occurring events:

Unholy Dying (November 1945)
Take Thee a Sharp Knife (February 1946)
Adventure with a Goat (April 1946, published as a double volume with *Apollo Wore a Wig*)
Bodies in a Bookshop (April 1946)
The Death Cap (June 1946)
Death for Madame (June 1946)
Swing Low, Swing Death (July 1946, published as a double volume with *The Death Cap*)

One of the most attractive features of the novels is they are alive with atmosphere—primarily of London in the 1940s. Todd did not dream up his backgrounds; he drew on his own experiences. Thus, *Unholy Dying* is set in the midst of a congress of geneticists, an environment he had recently experienced firsthand when helping his father-in-law, Francis Crew, himself a distinguished geneticist, to organize the Seventh International Congress of Genetics at Edinburgh University. His first draft of the story (then called *Drugs Fit and Time Agreeing*) was written in 1940, although it did not see publication until 1945. Also in 1940, Todd began writing *When the Bad Bleed*, which he never completed. However, the manuscript survives and leaves no doubt that this was an early version of *Take Thee a Sharp Knife*. This is a sleazy tale of murder in London's Soho and was based on his own all too frequent trips in the company of Dylan Thomas and other hard-drinking cronies around the bars and clubs of Soho and Fitzrovia. *Adventure with a Goat* is the shortest and slightest of the Stubbs novels, whose theme was suggested to him by an incident during childhood when a goat devoured the notes for a local minister's Sunday sermon before it could be delivered. *Bodies in a Bookshop* is a biblio-mystery, and Todd himself was a bibliomaniac who continually trawled the secondhand bookshops of Charing Cross Road to supplement his already groaning bookshelves. From childhood, Todd had been fascinated by the natural world and developed a specialized appreciation of fungi. Drawing on this knowledge, the plot of *The Death Cap* deals with the dastardly poisoning of a young woman using *amanita phalloides*, the deadly "death cap" mushroom. The plot of *Death for Madame* centers around the murder of the owner of a seedy residential hotel, inspired by Todd's dealings with the memorable Rosa Lewis, chef and owner of Cavendish Hotel in St. James's district of London. At the time he wrote the Stubbs novels, Todd was deeply occupied with art historical research, and his understanding of the world of art and artists provided him with the backdrop for *Swing Low, Swing Death*, a book in which a poet called Ruthven Todd makes a cameo appearance! We are lucky that Todd even left a clue in his memoirs about the plot of one of the four missing novels. Its events took place in a "progressive" school, a setting suggested no doubt by his interest in the work of A. S. Neill, founder of Summerhill School, which Todd had visited.

What do we know of Ruthven Campbell Todd himself? He was born in Edinburgh, Scotland, in 1914, the eldest of ten children of Walker Todd, an architect, and his wife, Christian. Ruthven received an elite private school education at Fettes College, which he hated and reacted against, leading to him being "asked to leave." During a short spell at Edinburgh College of Art, he recalled that he spent more time drinking beer and Crabbie's whiskey than attending to his studies. After less than a year, his father became fed up with his son's antics and Ruthven was dispatched to the Isle of Mull in the Scottish Highlands to work as a farm laborer for two years. After a further year as assistant editor to an obscure literary magazine, he left finally for London. Apart from occasional family visits, he never returned to Scotland.

In London, Todd embraced the bohemian world of poets, writers, and artists with rather too much enthusiasm, developing the alcoholism and addiction to strong tobacco that was to undermine his health and, to an extent, his productivity as a writer. Nevertheless, at this time he did publish several volumes of poetry as well as two fantasy novels, *Over the Mountain* and *The Lost Traveller* (the latter became something of a cult classic). His most notable achievement, however, was *Tracks in the Snow*, a book on Blake and his circle, which is still remembered today as a highly original and groundbreaking work.

In 1947, Todd left for the United States to pursue research for a complete catalog of the artworks of Blake. He lived there for the next thirteen years, first in New York City and later in Martha's Vineyard, Massachusetts. Here he became famous among younger readers for his four books about a feline astronaut, Space Cat, and he became a US citizen. In the late 1950s, he was commissioned to write the official life of Dylan Thomas, a project he failed to deliver. In 1960, while visiting Robert Graves in Mallorca, Spain, he became seriously ill with pleurisy and pneumonia and was hospitalized. He recovered, but the treatment costs he incurred meant he was unable to return to the United States. He lived in Mallorca for the rest of his life, first in Palma and then in the mountain village of Galilea, where he died of emphysema in 1978.

Original editions of Todd's detective novels remain elusive and expensive. However, Dover Publications is publishing four of the Stubbs books: *Bodies in a Bookshop; Unholy Dying; Swing Low, Swing Death;* and *Death for Madame.*

Peter Main, author
A Fervent Mind: The Life of Ruthven Todd
London, England, 2018

BODIES IN A
BOOKSHOP

Chapter 1

Booked for Murder

I DON'T know what came over me. It wasn't as if there were not enough books in the house to begin with. There were books on the floor, books on all the tables, books on the beds—and in the beds if one wasn't careful. Only that morning I had removed three volumes of Curtis from my room. How they came to be there I would not know. There seems to be a plot between the old man, Professor John Stubbs, and his housekeeper, Mrs. Farley, to dump anything they like in my room. So far as I am concerned this is fine. I like books. I like mess. But I have books enough and mess enough of my own.

Anyhow I had gone out with the intention of buying a book. It wasn't that I wanted any book. I had made up my mind. I wanted to read Louis Trenchard More's life of my famous namesake, Robert Boyle, the father of chemistry and uncle of the Earl of Cork.

I went to Zwemmer's Charing Cross Road. I found the book had been published in America and was out of stock, so I crawled up Gower Street, to see if there was an odd copy left in H. K. Lewis's. There wasn't.

Having made up my mind that I wanted the life of Robert Boyle I started going round all the bookshops I could find. This was fine, but I kept on running into other books I wanted. I spent the devil of a lot of money. I said to myself that it didn't really matter very much if I failed to get the *Life of Boyle*, I had gathered enough to keep me reading for at least a fortnight.

The old man had resigned himself to the thought that I was to take a fortnight's holiday. In three days I was going to the Scilly Isles to lie in the sun and enjoy a bit of quiet life, well out of reach of letters and telegrams. I had warned the old man that I would reply to neither. So far as he and the rest of the world were concerned I was going into retreat. I wished to be thought of as dead or hibernating for a fortnight.

1

The Professor had grumbled a bit when he realised that I actually meant to go away. I think he thought that I had been bluffing. But he had no legitimate cause for discontent. I was due for a holiday and he knew it.

The trouble with bookshops is that they are as bad as pubs. You start with one and then you drift to another, and before you know where you are you are on a gigantic book-binge. My brief case was full to bursting and I had bundles of books under both arms. I was bowed down by the weight of them.

I made up my mind that I would visit one more shop before I went home. There was a curious little shop in a side-street off the Tottenham Court Road, off the wrong side—towards Charlotte Street and the dismal bohemia, not towards the University and the eager students. I could never remember the name of the proprietor, but he sometimes had nice books which were not commonly in demand and his prices were always reasonable.

Sometimes I had bought books there so cheaply that I wondered what on earth the old fellow lived upon. He could not make a profit out of the shop. As a rule when I went there I was the only customer in the shop, so it didn't look as though business flourished.

I retraced my steps up the Charing Cross Road, having dumped my purchases in David Low's bookshop in Cecil Court.

I entered the little shop. It was piled to the ceiling with books. It reminded me faintly of the Professor's house in that the bookshelves had long before given up the effort to contain all the books. The only difference was that here the books were covered with dust while at home the indefatigable Mrs. Farley managed to keep the dust at bay by some magical means known only to herself.

I didn't see the proprietor when I entered the shop, but there was nothing unusual in that. He was probably in his back-room making up accounts or brewing himself a cup of tea on the rusty old gas-ring which I knew was there. I glanced towards the door. It was closed. I supposed he must be dealing with some business, so I decided to take myself on a voyage of discovery among the masses of books.

There was no denying it. The place *was* dusty. I got filthy, but I made some rather nice finds. Books which I had hoped to obtain some-time kept on peering out at me as I disturbed the cobwebs and the grey brown London dust. I found a nice copy of the first collected edition of the works of Sir Thomas Browne and a copy of Erasmus Darwin's *Phytologia or the Philosophy of Agriculture*, with a presentation inscription to that amiable bore, William Hayley. I laid these aside and went on with my quest.

I suppose I spent about an hour and a half nosing among the piles of ancient calf-bound books. Some of those I laid aside would need some attention from the binder, but the prices scribbled upon the fly-leaves were so ridiculously small that I could not resist them.

The dust I raised in my hunt was so thick that I sneezed and coughed a good deal.

I suppose that must have been the reason that I did not notice an alien smell until I was looking through the books just beside the entrance to the private room, where the old man kept his treasures and his desk.

Once I did notice it, I paid little attention to it for a few minutes. There was no reason why I should. It was only the smell of ordinary household gas and I suppose I had a subconscious memory of that rusty old gas-ring and the smell it distilled in the room.

I was looking at a copy of William Derham's *Physico-Theology*, 1713. It needed repairing, but the price was reasonable considering that it was a presentation copy from the author and that he had filled the end-papers with additional notes in a neat crabbed hand before giving it to his friend, Benjamin Lane, whoever he might be. I placed it on my pile, which had begun to assume pyramidical proportions.

As I turned round it struck me that the smell was stronger than it should have been. I walked up to the door of the back room and tried the handle. It turned all right but the door refused to open. I gave it a heave, but it still seemed to be stuck. I wondered whether the proprietor would be annoyed with me for intruding upon his privacy.

I was just about to kick at the lock, for I was beginning to feel rather worried, when I noticed that the door was fastened shut with a bolt at the top.

That was the solution. The old man had gone out and had forgotten to turn off the gas or to lock up the shop. He had, however, remembered to bolt the back room where he kept his money in a drawer of the desk, but hadn't realised that anyone could walk in and take it by merely unbolting the door.

I wondered what I should do. I decided that I would be doing no harm by going into the room and turning off the gas. The old proprietor would remember my face and not suspect me of burglarous intentions if he came in and found me engaged in breaking into his private room.

I slid the bolt back and opened the door. The gust of gas that caught me in the face drove me backwards. I went to the door of the shop and took a deep breath of fresh air. I turned round and advanced boldly into the back-room, with my mind set on the gas ring. I reached it in a couple of strides and grabbed the turn-cock. It wouldn't turn.

I was so intent on my struggle with the little bit of dull and tarnished brass that it wasn't until I had practically exhausted my breath that I looked at the rest of the room. When I did I damned nearly gasped. The room was not as I had expected, unoccupied. Not only was the old proprietor lying on the floor, but there was another man with him. I stooped down and grabbed them by their coat-collars and started to drag them out of the room. The proprietor was light enough, but the other man was a bit heavier. However I made it. I knocked down one of the tall piles of dusty volumes as I heaved them into the outer shop.

I managed to get them near the door. I took a deep breath of good clean air, for my lungs were nearly bursting and I had a tight band of metal frozen across my skull. I turned to deal with the two men I had pulled out of the room.

It was obvious that I could not hope to give artificial respiration to both of them. On second thoughts it seemed unlikely that any artificial respiration would be of use. Their faces were suffused to the colour of well-boiled lobsters.

All the same, it was up to me to do my best. I looked out of the shop again. There was no one in sight. I didn't know what to do. Then I remembered that, down one side of the shop, there ran an alley, with its mouth in Charlotte Street. The Charlotte Street end being wider than that in Wesley Street, a thoughtful post-office had erected a public telephone. I ran down the alley.

I got hold of the police and told them what had happened as quickly as possible. I suppose that by the time I had finished talking an ambulance was ready to set out. I rang off.

Of course it was none of my business, but I thought I had better do something more about it. I rang up Scotland Yard and asked if Chief Inspector Reginald E. Bishop was available. He was.

"I say, Bishop," I said, "I seem to have stumbled into a bit more death."

His voice was weary as he answered me, "You would. What is it this time?"

I told him.

"It seems queer to me that the room should be bolted on the outside and the men inside be sitting there inhaling gas, doesn't it? So far as I could see they had made no efforts to get out, but were lying quite quietly on the floor."

"Yes, Boyle," he said listlessly, "I'm afraid I'll need to look into it. Tell the Divisional Inspector what you've told me and that you've been in communication with me. Stay there till I arrive if you can."

He rung off and I wandered back towards the shop. As I arrived at the narrow-end of the alley I heard the clang of an ambulance bell.

There was no doubt about it. Both men were dead. Very dead. I had a better chance to look at them before they were taken away. The old proprietor whose name, it turned out was Allan Leslie, was a small, grey-haired man. In life his cheeks had been as rosy as a Cox's Orange Pippin. I had sometimes wondered how he had managed to look so healthy shut in the dust and mould of nearly a hundred thousand books.

The other man was not tall, but rather broad. Papers in his pocket gave his name as Cecil Baird. His clothes were in rather better condition than those of old Leslie, who did not seem to have been aware that the ends of his trousers had become frayed or that his elbows shewed grimy patches of lining. Baird seemed to have been a man of some substance. Among the contents of his pockets were a gold watch and a gold propelling pencil. His well-filled pocket-book was made of pigskin with gold corners. His dark hair had been receding from the crown of his head.

A small crowd had gathered from nowhere and was standing around the ambulance as the stretcher-bearers carried the bodies out, covered with blankets. A smart-looking youngish man came into the shop. He conversed quietly with the constable who had taken charge.

While they were talking I suddenly realised that there was something strange. It was as if a clock had suddenly stopped. I listened for a moment to see if I could identify the feeling that I had. Then I realised what it was. The gas had ceased. All the time I had been aware of the faint hissing in the background. I had explained to the constable my inability to turn off the turn-cock but he did not seem to pay much attention to my remarks. He had made no effort to turn off the gas himself. Now it had stopped of its own accord.

I was angry with myself. Why the hell I hadn't been content to go home with the books I'd left at Low's I did not know. It was as bad as dipsomania this book-buying, and its results were even more startling. It looked to me as though I had landed myself in the devil of a mess. Just when I was going on holiday, too. The old man would chortle like hell and try and make it an excuse for me to postpone my holiday, but I was damned if I would.

I knew I hadn't the hope of an ice-cream in hell of keeping him away from this. He would be in it up to the neck. I knew he would get into trouble. But it was none of my business. He could get himself into trouble and out again without my help. After all he had been doing it for years before I became his assistant, so it wouldn't be a bad thing for the Professor to have to do without me once again.

The Divisional Inspector, for so the young man proved to be, came across and introduced himself to me.

"My name is Potter," he said, "Mr — — er . . ."

"Boyle," I supplied obligingly, "Max Boyle."

"I believe that you discovered this distressing affair, and that it was you who telephoned for the ambulance? Now I would like to hear from you exactly what happened? Don't hurry yourself, but try to tell it in your own words as simply and directly as possible."

I told him. He walked into the inside room, which was beginning to clear, took a look at the gas-ring and then came back again. He looked puzzled.

"You say, Mr. Boyle," he asked, "that the room was bolted on the *outside*? Yes? That's very odd, isn't it?"

I agreed that it was indeed very odd.

"It's a great pity, of course, Mr. Boyle, that you had to interfere with the things inside the room. Not that I'm blaming you, mind, but it would perhaps have given us a lead if things had been left as you found them. Oh, I know you only thought that old Leslie had gone out and the flame on the gas had been extinguished by accident, and then, when you saw the bodies, you did what anyone would have done. I'd have tried to do it myself. All the same it is a pity, a very great pity."

A figure like a large and well-fed Persian cat suddenly materialised in the door of the shop. It was Chief Inspector Bishop. Beneath a black homburg his eyes looked weary. He would have scowled at me but that it would have required too much energy.

"Hullo, Max," he said slowly, "I see you're in trouble again. If I had my way both you and the Professor would be serving life sentences. That would be the only way to keep you out of mischief. Though," his voice was tired, "I suppose that even on Dartmoor the Professor would find some trouble to run into."

I was mad.

"Look here, Sir," I said, "Do you think I go around inviting people to die off more or less on my doorstep? Do you think I like being mixed up with murder? I like a quiet life as well as you do. I am a botanist and not a blinking detective. I was quietly buying books and this happens to me. I want to go away on holiday and I get tied up."

If I had been any angrier I would have had apoplexy.

Chapter 2

Death by Gas

MY TEMPER rose like boiling milk in a saucepan. I spluttered with indignation. The Bishop smiled at me. It was obvious I could not get under his skin. He seemed to have suffered everything before and was consequently imperturbable. Rage as I might he just looked bored.

I had just about worked my temper out when I heard a familiar noise outside in Wesley Street. It was the Professor swearing at his car. This was indeed the end. I'd had enough. I wanted to go away and die.

The old man entered the shop. He was wearing an immense moth-eaten sombrero stuck on the top of his head. It was rather too small for him. He had once told me that it had been left behind by a plant-physiologist from the Middle West, who had visited him to discuss some problems of rust-resistant wheat and who had succumbed to the brandy and long hours of talk. The man had gone away with a head like a steeple and had felt he couldn't reach the top of it, so he had left the hat behind. Professor Stubbs fancied himself in this hat. His grey hair sprouted around the edge of it. His steel-rimmed glasses were perched on the end of his nose, blunt as the end of his thumb. He beamed at us and peered out between the top of his glasses and his bushy eyebrows. He was as amiable as Napoleon brandy. I glowered at him.

"'Ullo, Max," he boomed cheerfully, "findin' more bodies for me to play wi,' eh? That's the boy."

"How the hell, why the likewise did you get here or are you here?" I howled in a muddled way.

He pursed his lips and tried to look mysterious, but saw that I was really annoyed.

"Oh," his voice was as airy as Hyde Park, "the Chief Inspector who always has me best interests at heart, rang me up an' told me that ye'd been gettin' into a bit o' trouble, so I came rushin' along as fast as I could to get ye out o' it. I got a kindly character. That's me trouble. I can't let me assistant get into trouble wi' out tryin' to help him out o' it."

I looked at the Chief Inspector. His face betrayed that the old man was telling the truth. I could cheerfully have tied the two of them together in a sack and drowned them in the Serpentine.

"I was spending a quiet and pleasing afternoon," I said coldly, "in the harmless occupation of spending more money than I could afford on some books, and by pure bad luck I walk smack into the middle of a tragedy. Am I to be held responsible for this? Am I to suffer for my public spiritedness in ringing up the police? I could have gone away and said nothing. I could have taken my books and gone home. My social conscience however forbade this course, so I suffer."

I put as much clotted misery into my voice as I could. I might just have well have recited Hamlet's soliloquy. Neither of them paid the least attention to my pleas.

The Chief Inspector asked me a great many questions. Like the Divisional Inspector he regretted that I had touched so much. I grew more and more angry. I had suddenly realised that I was not to be able to remove my collection of nice books. I would need to wait until the whole business of the death of old Leslie had been sorted out before I could apply to his heirs or executors.

The Professor lit his filthy pipe. He lumbered about the bookshop. He pulled down books absentmindedly, ruffled their pages, and replaced them upside down. I had tried to cure him of this habit, but in vain.

"You are sure, Max," the Bishop asked wearily, "that the door was bolted? Could it not have been that it was jammed and your assault upon it had loosened it at the same moment that you noticed the bolt? Perhaps it was pushed a bit of the way over, but had not caught, and in your hurry you thought it was holding and pulled it back, without actually making any difference to the actual bolting of the door."

I was sure. I had had to give the bolt a bit of a tug to get it open. I knew that the bolt had been holding all right. I said so, perhaps rather forcibly.

"All right," the Chief Inspector was consolatory, "I'll take your word for it that it was bolted. But I still can't see why it had been bolted."

"Hah," the old man advanced upon the Bishop like a heavy charger, "perhaps it was bolted by one of the dead men."

"Yes," the Chief Inspector was weary, "who then spirited himself through it and lay down beside the other and inhaled the gas. Not, if I may say so, *very* likely."

He accentuated the word *very* to the point where it became the appropriate swear-word.

Professor Stubbs was not the least bit abashed.

"No," he rumbled, "I got a mechanical mind. I read thrillers. There's thousands o' ways in which ye can bolt a door from the other side—wi' pencils an' bits o' string an' levers an' whatnot. No doubt I could do it meself."

I put my oar in heavily.

"Go and try it," I said bitterly, "just you go and try it. I'll bet you can't. I opened the bolt and I know. It was stiff."

Professor Stubbs lumbered heavily over to the door. He tried the bolt once or twice experimentally. Flakes of rust crumbled off it as he slid it backwards and forwards. He shook his head sadly and the sombrero slid down over his eyes. He was not disconcerted. He took it off and jammed it heavily on the back of his head, where it gave him the appearance of having the halo of a fallen angel.

"Umhum," he grunted heavily, "I'm afraid ye're right, Max, for once in yer life. I don't know how it could be done."

He scowled at the Chief Inspector and scratched his head with a blunt finger, tangling the hair that escaped from the hat. He took out his beastly little pipe, made of black congo wood in the shape of a penny clay pipe. He swore that it had dripped tar when he had smoked it in, but that was so long ago that his memory might have been at fault.

From one waistcoat pocket he dug a piece of thick dark brown twist which he proceeded to shred into his hand with a tiny ladylike pearl-handled knife he kept for the purpose. He rubbed the grains and fragments of tobacco between his hands and tilted them into the pipe. He tamped the load down with a square thumb and put a light to it with an immense petrol-lighter which flared like a volcano.

Once his head was comfortably swathed in vile, grey smoke, adding to his resemblance to a bulky Miltonic fallen angel, he beamed at us.

It is impossible to deter the old man for long. He has as much bounce as a squash-ball.

"Now," he grumbled, "we've decided that the door couldn't ha' bin bolted from the inside, we got to think why it was bolted from the outside. It can't ha' bin to prevent those inside escapin', for if they'd wanted to they could ha' broken the glass in the window, wi' any handy object."

He picked up a heavy blackthorn stick from the corner of the inner room. It was of the sort known as a shillelagh.

"Somethin' like this," he grumbled, laying it down again, "an' ye see no attempt has bin made to break the glass. No, it beats me. I can't for the life o' me see the reason for bolting the door on the outside like that. It's yer move, Bishop, let's see what ye make o' it. Can ye give us a reasonable explanation?"

The Chief Inspector looked at him in a tired fashion.

"You know as well as I do, John," he complained, "that I can't go around inventing theories and discarding them at the rate at which you do it. I am a slow and careful man and I take all things into consideration before I dare deduce anything from the facts. I abhor theory without facts, and as a policeman I am forced to eschew such fancy completely. Thank God!"

Professor Stubbs grinned.

"Good old stick-in-the-mud," he said rudely, "won't risk an opinion on anythin' till it's bin handed to him on a plate an' he's had a chance to taste an' smell it, an' even then he waits for a month in case he should develop food poisonin' Yah!"

It seemed to me that I was about to witness a Box and Cox cross-talk display, with rude patter from the Professor and polite explanation from the Chief Inspector.

However, the Bishop, moving sadly about the little inner room, came to a halt before the rusty old gas-ring. He picked it up and looked at it curiously. The old man stumped over to him and also took a look at it.

The Chief Inspector tried to twiddle the turn-cock. It refused to budge.

"Ah, yes, Max," he said, turning to me, "I see what you mean. It seems to have been jammed on."

"Gi' it to me," the old man grunted, "I got a mechanical mind. I'll see if I can turn it."

Professor Stubbs took hold of the rusty metal object. He also tried in vain to twist the little brass tap. He looked at if closely through his steel-rimmed glasses.

"Urr," he grumbled, "looks to me as though it hadn't worked for a long time. Here, take a dekko at it. See these flakes o' rust, well, what d'ye think?"

I moved up to the meeting of the sages and took a look. The Professor was quite right. The tap had not turned for a long time.

"But," I said in a puzzled way, "I've seen old Leslie boiling a kettle on that ring dozens of times. At least he always seemed to use that ring. Perhaps," a bright idea hit me, "someone has changed that ring for the one that worked?"

Professor Stubbs was down on all fours. He looked like a baby elephant crawling along the floor. He was examining the joint where the snaky gas tube joined a gas point on the wall. I looked down at him.

There was another tap at that gas point, or, at least, there had been. It had been broken off at sometime, flush with the top of the pipe. The break was not new. The brass was dark with exposure across the ragged break. It would have been impossible for anyone to turn the tap with his bare fingers.

However, Professor Stubbs paid little attention to the tap. He was examining the connection.

"Huh," he growled, looking up over his shoulder, "this joint ain't bin fiddled wi'. Look at the dirt on it. An' now you go an' take a look at the gas-ring, an' the place where the tube joins that. Ye'll see that that ain't bin touched either, eh?"

He was quite right. It was obvious that the tubing had been fixed firmly at both ends for a very long time. I looked along the tubing. There was no possibility that anyone had done a neat join in the middle of it to lead us astray. The tube was indubitably "all, all of a piece throughout."

"But," I insisted irritably, "how the hell do you explain the fact that I saw a kettle boiling on this ring? And, if it comes to that, where did the gas come from and why has it stopped?"

The old man hoisted himself from his knees. He paid no attention to the fact that he had gathered a considerable amount of dust while imitating Nebuchadnezzar. He beamed at me amiably. I scowled at him and waited for enlightenment.

"Ye're not what I'd call observant today, Max. The reason that the gas ceased to flow was that the money in the meter had run out. Didn't ye notice the meter outside the door? Eh?"

Thinking back I remembered having seen the meter. A grey-green box of a thing, about three feet into the shop. Subconsciously I had noted that it was not piled with books like everything else, but I had not given it another chance.

"Well, Max," the old man was pleased with himself, "suppose ye have a meter which ye feed wi' pennies, an' ye have a gas-ring which won't work at the taps, what d'ye think ye'd do when ye wanted to boil a kettle? Eh? Harrumph! I'll tell ye what ye'd do. Ye'd put a penny in the slot an' keep the gas lighted till the penny was finished, wouldn't ye? Eh? If ye'll look around ye'll see that the gas-fire in this room has bin disconnected, an' the connection plugged up. If ye'll look ye'll see that this hasn't bin done this afternoon. The lights are electric an' there's a little electric bowl-fire, quite enough to heat a man sittin' at the desk. So ye see that the only thin' that was run by the gas in the whole blinkin' shop was that gas-ring."

His face plainly said that Quod Erat had been damned well Demonstrandum. It was delightfully simple once it occurred to one. I could see that he was right.

The Chief Inspector looked at him thoughtfully, opening his sleepy eyes a trifle.

"Clever, John," he said, "clever. And what do you deduce from that? Have you anything else in the way of tricks up your sleeve."

Professor Stubbs looked about as modest as a tiger lily. He beamed with the utmost benevolence.

"Hum," he rumbled, "I wouldn't say it was clever. It was obvious. I just said to meself, 'Now, John, ye want to make yerself a cup o' tea, an' yer blinking gas-ring don't work so how do ye do it?' An' then I remembered seein' that meter outside the room an' so I knew the answer. Like Max, here, I'd noticed the meter when I was lookin' round, like him I hadn't taken it in. A gas meter's the sort o' thin' ye expect to find around where there's gas, so I didn't pay any attention to it. I just kinda assumed that the police had turned off the gas at the main. But then I saw it had to be a penny in the slot meter or otherwise the gas-ring would ha' had to run all the time."

He lumbered over to the door of the room and looked at the bolt again. He shut the door and slipped the bolt home with a harsh grating of rust. He opened the door again and looked at us.

"Yes," he said slowly, "what I'd say happened here was that Leslie an' Baird were in some way drugged, an' the murderer, who must ha' bin intimate wi' Leslie, went an' put a couple of bob in the meter, bolted the door on the outside in case they came to, an' walked off to leave 'em to die o' coal gas poisonin'. But that's as far as I can go. If ye're to ask me why this was done or why this method was chosen I'll have to admit that I'm stumped. There must ha' bin a reason for the choice o' method, but we'll need to find out a bit more before we can say anythin' about that. Eh?"

The Chief Inspector nodded wearily. There were still one or two police officials in the shop, testing surfaces for fingerprints and so on. They ran over the meter. There were plenty of blurred prints upon it, but, as the Bishop said, there was no doubt that they were all made by Leslie.

I got a bit of string off the desk in the inner room and tied my chosen books together gently. I did not see why I should allow the death of the old proprietor to interfere with the growth of my library. I inserted a slip with my name on it under the string. I would buy the books from whoever was executor or heir. No doubt everything would be cleared up by the time I returned from my holiday.

Chapter 3

Visit from a Lady

I HEARD a noise at the door of the shop. The constable on duty was talking to someone, a woman. She sounded agitated. There seemed to be some argument in progress.

The Chief Inspector strolled over to the door. He looked out.

"That's all right," he told the constable lazily.

The shop was entered by a small woman of about seventy. She could not have been any older, but her clothes belonged to a much earlier date. She wore a sort of turban hat pinned to the mathematical crown of her head. This hat was a remarkable piece of architecture. It seemed to have been the recipient of not only a harvest offering, but of the morgue of the ornithological department of the Zoo—feathers of love-birds and wings of ortlans disported themselves among bunches of artificial wheat, cherries and various flowers that never were on wayside or in woodland.

Beneath this hat there was a tight wad of iron grey hair. A little middle-aged face peered out below this. Small brown eyes set in crow's feet looked worried. A precise little mouth gaped slightly open in dismay.

Round her neck was an ostrich feather boa, a thing I hadn't seen since my grandmother died, donkey's years ago. The clothes were black and rustling.

"Well, madam," the Chief Inspector was enquiring but sympathetic, "what can I do for you?"

"Oh, isn't it dreadful?" the voice was gentle and quiet, "The policeman outside tells me that my uncle Allan has—ah—er—ah—passed over. What has happened?"

"I'm afraid, Madam," the Chief Inspector was obviously uncertain of how to approach the subject, "that Mr. Leslie is indeed dead. I take it that you are his niece?"

"Oh, yes, I'm his niece," the words were coming more easily, "and I keep house for him. My name is Alice Hortense Wright, Miss Wright. I always come round to see him whenever I'm up this way and sometimes we go home together."

"Harrumph," the Professor lumbered on to the scene, "Did he ever make ye a cup o' tea when ye came here?"

"Of course. Why not?"

"Um, did ye ever notice anythin' queer about the gas-ring?"

"No. Oh, wait a minute, I know what you mean. Yes. When he wanted to boil a kettle he used to put a penny in the meter and keep the gas-ring going until the penny had been spent. I was always telling him to buy a new gas-ring. It wasted so much money having to wait till the gas was exhausted. But he would never bother about it and I'm afraid I put off buying one myself, as I didn't know if he would use it if I did give it to him. Uncle Allan is inclined to be hot tempered and he resents interference."

She paused. The use of the present tense had suddenly dawned on her in its incongruity.

"Oh," she gasped into a small lace-fringed handkerchief, "but what has all this to do with Uncle Allan's—er—?" This time she faced the word *death*.

Gently but precisely, the Chief Inspector told her what had happened. She took it well, dabbing occasionally at her eyes with the scrap of handkerchief. I had expected that we would have to deal with a hysterical woman, but there was none of that about Miss Wright. She was certainly upset, but she had herself well under control.

"Now, Miss Wright," the Bishop said when he had finished his list of happenings, "if you don't mind I would like to ask one or two questions. First, I gather that you kept house for your uncle? Where do you live?"

"Fourteen Allery Street?" she replied, "it's in Streatham, you know. Not very far from Brixton, where all the big stores were till they got bombed." She shuddered at the recollection of the bombing.

"Now, do you know whether your uncle had any enemies? What do you know about Mr. Baird," he looked at his notes, "Mr. Cecil Baird?"

"As I've already said, my uncle was a hot-tempered man who resented anything that seemed like interference with his own concerns. I am quite sure that he must have offended a great many people, particularly people in the book-trade, but none of them would have done this. Oh, no, of course they wouldn't. I think that even the people whom he had offended liked my uncle in spite of his crabbiness. He was looked upon in the trade as a man who knew his subjects and who was usually right in the end. And, of course, he was usually charming and very nice to people. He offended some customers because if there was one thing he couldn't stand, it was for someone to try and buy a book for less than he had marked it. He was very rude to people who tried to offer for books. He would roar at them to take their custom elsewhere to—" she named a large emporium, usually known as "the grocery of the book-trade," "if they wanted to haggle. His prices were fair and he did not like the bargain-hunter!"

I agreed with what she had said, for I never argued about the prices of old Leslie's books, and I had seen him being rude to a man who had tried to have sixpence knocked off a price. He had always been charming to me.

"Mr. Baird," she went on, "was an acquaintance of my uncle's. I don't think he liked him much, but I think he found him useful in connection with his book-buying. He came to dinner with us once or twice. He was very well-spoken and amusing, but always seemed to be thinking of something else."

I thought I could see these little brown bird-eyes, watching and making mental notes. Quite obviously Miss Wright was as astute as her uncle was supposed to have been.

Professor Stubbs had stumped back into the private room. He was perched on a chair in front of Leslie's desk and, with a complete disregard for the Chief Inspector's glances, was engaged in wading through the papers which were gathered there. I wandered over and took a look at them.

There were bundles of other booksellers' catalogues and back numbers of the booksellers' trade paper, the *Clique*. There were report cards from all over the country and various letters from customers, ordering or asking for specific books.

Like a man sweeping up leaves, the old man brushed most of these aside. I looked at them when they were rejected, but could get nothing of any interest out of them. Under the Professor's large square left hand, however, I noticed that there was a small pile of papers gathering. He had them hidden so that I could not see what they contained, but I could make out that they were all letters and that there were no postcards among them.

There seemed to be no future in playing Peeping Tom over the old man's shoulder, so I sat down on a pile of books and thumbed my way through some numbers of the *Clique*. I had never seen it before so I was interested to learn that this was the way in which booksellers communicated with one another and that when one said, "Oh, I'll advertise for it, sir, and see if I can get a copy," he meant that he would advertise in the *Clique*. Apart from the long lists of books wanted by booksellers from Inverness to Penzance, there were other interesting little notes— warnings about book-thieves, notices that should certain books be offered for sale they were stolen, and so on.

I heard the Chief Inspector dismissing Miss Wright and looked up. He came into the back room looking as weary as always. The old man paid no attention to him. He sat at the desk grunting to himself.

"Hullo, John," the Bishop was almost friendly, "what are you up to? Have you found that old Leslie was the centre of a gang of criminals? The master-mind sitting in the middle of his webs?"

With distaste the Chief Inspector flicked a cob-web between two piles of books beside him. The old man looked up. His face was stretched into a smile. He ran a blunt finger into his tangled hair and leaned back, almost upsetting the chair he was perched on.

"Um," he rumbled slowly, "while I ain't found that Leslie was a master-crook, I found somethin' almost as interestin'. If ye'll look at these letters I got here under me hand, ye'll see that he did a very flourishin' little business in the seamier sort o' literature. These are all orders for pornographic books, an' when he had supplied the book that was wanted, Leslie very obligin'ly wrote the price against it. Here, for example, is a copy o' an English translation o' Sade's *Justine*—it's a dam' bad translation, too. Well, Leslie got fifty quid for that."

He beamed again. The Chief Inspector looked at him severely.

"I didn't know that you went in for that kind of thing, John?" he said, "Yet here you are able to criticise the translation of an obscene book."

"Uhhuh," the old man nodded, "I read it, as I read anythin' that I come across, from bus-tickets to the Oxford Dictionary. It was a stinkin' translation an' dam' funny. It must ha' bin done about the eighteen eighties an' the language at that time wasn't suitable for bein' dirty in. I wouldn't ha' given a shillin' for the book meself, but here's someone wantin' it bad enough to pay all that money. Um."

He pursed his lips together and looked at us. His expression said plainly that he considered that there were a great many fools in the world and that, in looking through Leslie's papers, he felt that he had become the cuckoo in a veritable fool's nest.

"Pah! But that's not all. I don't know enough about the trade, or about old books, but from certain indications here I think ye'll find that Leslie did a flourishin' business in stolen books too. None of your ordinary stealin' either, but books worth in the region o' hundreds o' pounds, books which a collector might covet, but which he would need to keep hidden. Rummy game that, buyin' a book an' gloatin' over it in private. When ye come to think o' it, ye'll see that the man who'd buy a book wi' a doubtful history in order to look at it an' fondle it all to himself, is not so very different from the feller who buys the pornography an' treats it in the same way."

He thumped the desk with his closed fist and the papers jumped and rustled. The Chief Inspector moved languidly towards the Professor and looked down at the papers, which the old man was spreading out again.

He picked up a few of the letters and read them quickly. His face shewed his distaste for anyone who would meddle with pornography.

"Ye see," the old man grunted, "that the orders are for the out o' the way kinda pornography, not for the common banned book or slightly off kinda novel? There seems to ha' bin some money in that, judging from the notes. Here's one o' these little Japanese books o' woodcuts. A good one too, none o' yer modern trash designed to catch the pennies o' the tourist. Ye'll see that Leslie has two notes o' prices on it? I suppose, an' I'm probably right, that the smaller one is what he gave for the book, an' the large what he received. If that's the case, he gave a tenner for it an' hauled in a tidy little sum of two-fifty."

The Chief Inspector laid down the papers. He looked very thoughtful. His eyes were half-shut.

"Um, yes," he said slowly, "and I suppose you realise, John, that the man who sold these things was in a good position to indulge in a little blackmail on the side—particularly in the case of the stolen books. Of course, he would not be able to do it himself. To do that would be to wring the neck of the golden goose, but, say, Leslie had a partner who worked that end of the business, they could manage fairly well. Yes. I'm afraid that is something which I'll have to look into. The trouble is that I'm going to make myself damned unpopular with a lot of psychopathic idiots who have a perfectly harmless desire to read dirt, and I'm going to have to clean out the whole of this business to see who the stolen books really belong to."

He looked very unhappy.

"You can clear out what you like," I said, "but these books tied up with string belong to me. I would have paid for them and have had them home by now if the old fool hadn't gone and got himself murdered. Anyhow, I'm thirsty and I see the pubs should be open by now. You can go on filling your lungs with dust and the air with hotter air. I'm going for a drink."

The Chief Inspector went on looking pretty moody. No drink on earth would have cheered him, but the old man straightened up. He usually does this slowly, but he did it fairly fast. He looked at me with real pleasure.

"Thank'ee, Max," he roared, "I knew there was somethin' wrong, but I couldn't place it off hand. Me stomach's bin dehydratin' for hours an' needs a little moisture. Where are we goin'?"

Since we were on the fringe, the lunatic fringe, of the sordid bohemia, I suggested we should go slumming and visit one of their pubs. I felt pretty doubtful about taking the old man anywhere. The last time I'd taken him out for an evening's quiet drinking we had walked straight into a murder.

However, I felt I'd had the daily ration of sudden death and felt pretty safe. It was unlikely that we would run into more trouble. I took him to the *Fitzroy*, or rather he took me in that damned old Bentley which frightens the guts out of me. The old man looked with pleasure at the caricatures of old Kleinfeld and Charlie Alchild on the walls. He read all the messages on the posters of the 1914–18 war, Kitchener looking threatening and stale slogans, "Will you March first, or wait till March First?" "Your King and Country needs you!" all mercifully dulled down by the yellowing varnish.

There was a big fire at the far end of the bar, and the old man placed himself beside it. I fed him with beer. I put a penny in the slot on the counter and let the player-piano go through its antics. This machine fascinated him and he spent two shillings on it; his inclination was to overstuff it with pennies.

Finally, I got him seated again. The locals were drifting into the pub. Young men with corduroy trousers and dirty feet shewing between the leather straps of sandals were accompanied by girls whose style of hairdressing did not seem to have altered since the days of Katherine Mansfield. I introduced the old man to Nina Hamnett. They got on very well. I never knew he had such a fund of stories. Nina drifted off. She had to do a drawing of someone.

The old man beamed at me.

"Why the hell," he enquired gustily, "didn't you bring me here before? It's a fine place. Why do you keep all yer dives to yerself?"

I replied that perhaps I wanted a quiet life and didn't go round these places as often as I had when I was a student. He engulfed quite a lot of beer before he reverted to the subject of the murder.

"Look here," I said. I was stern, "I'm not interested in anything to do with murder. I'm going on holiday and I am unwilling to think of anything except the sun and the sea. You can dabble in the case if you like. I won't help you."

Chapter 4

Alibi on Anonymity

I MIGHT just as well have given up without a struggle. I should have had the sense to know I couldn't win. The old man weighs more than three of me in the balance and I hadn't a chance. I sent a telegram to the Scilly Isles, cancelling my booking of rooms.

I do not think that you could describe breakfast as a matey meal. I sat there and glowered at the fringe of black grounds in the bottom of my coffee cup. The old man was cheerful enough. He was wrapped in his immense tartan dressing gown and looked like something left over from the novels of Sir Walter Scott, which had been hibernating for a hundred years and had not improved in the time. I unwrapped my post, two catalogues from booksellers, Davis & Orioli and Wheldon & Wesley.

As a rule I would have gone through these catalogues with the utmost care, but this morning I felt that I'd had enough of booksellers. I laid them aside, reflecting that by the time I came to look at them everything I wanted would have gone and that it would probably be as well for my pocket if that happened.

"Harrumph," the old man exploded suddenly across the table, "Well, we got a nice murder on our hand, ain't we?" He looked as pleased as if he had arranged the murder and carried it out himself. I did not look encouraging. He was faintly apologetic as he went on, "O' course, Max, it's a bit tough for you, havin' to postpone yer holiday like this, but as good a murder as this don't come our way every day o' the week, do it?"

I reflected that the Professor's grammar was getting more slipshod every day and I said so. I might as well have tried to stop a tank with a peashooter. He beamed at me as amiably as a stuffed panda.

"I've already told you that I wish to have nothing to do with any murders," I said acidly, "if you wish to tie yourself up with them that's your business, but I won't help you. I've given up my holiday to try to let you run around while I attend to such business as needs attention. But—murder—no—murder is beyond my scope. I want a quiet life and I'll try to get it."

He paid no attention to me. A wedge of toast with Oxford marmalade was washed down with coffee.

"Trouble is," he was irrepressible, "that we got so dam' little to go on. Here we have Leslie, a dealer in pornography an' stolen books, gettin' himself murdered in the company o' a gent called Baird about whom we know nothin' except that there was some business connection between 'em. The fact that they were done in together suggests that maybe there was some illegal connection between 'em, unless, o' course, the murderer had to bump off Baird for security reasons."

I could see the clockwork of his brain was ticking like a metronome. If I wasn't careful I would be hauled in as his Watson once again; I have no liking for playing Watson to the old man's Sherlock. I haven't the right kind of mind. I am not suitably astonished when he produces the solution like the rabbit from the conjuror's topper. Much as I admire the Professor I have to confess that he irritates me almost beyond endurance. I dare say this comes out as I write. I spend the whole of any of his murder cases in a state of bottled wrath, and not too securely bottled at that.

After I had finished breakfast I went out to the garden. I was nursing some seedlings he had brought from Kew. My private opinion is that he goes round and snaffles anything he wants.

About eleven o'clock Professor Stubbs came lumbering down the path towards me. My temper had cooled down considerably so I looked at him if not with pleasure at least with tolerance. He saw this and looked at me with the affability of a polar bear regarding its lunch.

"Comin' wi' me?" he asked. "I'm goin' to visit Reggie Bishop. I just rang him up an' he told me to come along."

"All right," I was ungracious, "I'll come with you and try to keep you out of trouble."

The old Bentley bucked and bounced its way towards Whitehall. I felt the pigment dying out of my hair at every corner. It won't be the old man's fault if I'm not snow-white by the time I'm forty.

The Chief Inspector sat behind his desk. His face was as weary as I'd ever seen it. Before him were spread the papers we had last seen lying on Leslie's desk. He looked up at us through half-closed eyes.

"Damn you, Max," he said mildly, "I feel that you go out of your way to give me difficult cases. I feel sure that murderers lie in wait round corners and tell themselves that you or John are coming and then prepare a murder that has no apparent rhyme or reason for its existence. Give me a nice straightforward gang murder, or robbery with violence, and then I know where I am."

"Bah!" the old man was violent, "trouble wi' you, Reggie, is ye're getting fat an' don't like anythin' that disturbs the even tenor o' yer ways. Come on now. Tell us where ye got to. What's the result o' burnin' the midnight oil? Eh?"

"Sweet damn all," the Bishop spread his hands with a gesture that might have passed as a benediction, "here we are with an apparently harmless bookseller and a man of what they call 'independent means' murdered. Then it appears that the bookseller was engaged in illegal activities, but not activities that would account for his murder. I have been trying to prepare a list of his principal associates. They are a book-sellers' runner called Ellis Read. A bookseller in Fulham called Charles Hume. A bookseller from Bristol of the name of Ronald Hunter and a printseller called Henry Gray. I have not yet had time to question any of these people, but I have discovered that Hunter is in town."

The Professor had just planted himself in a chair from which he over-flowed on all sides. He hoisted himself to his feet again. His face had the pleased look of a child who was about to be taken to a pantomime.

"Goin' visitin', eh?" he enquired in a voice full of glee "I'm comin' wi' ye. Who're ye goin' to call on first? Eh? The Hunter man? That's the stuff. I'll run ye there in me car."

The Chief Inspector seemed shaken by the prospect, but to my surprise he accepted the Professor's offer.

Ronald Hunter was staying in a small hotel off Russell Square. I thought we were about to crash when the old man spotted a grey squirrel on one of the plane trees in the square and howled at me to look at it, gesturing towards it with both hands. The Chief Inspector manfully resisted the temptation to seize the wheel and by some miracle the Professor regained control.

The Chief Inspector rang the bell at the hotel door and asked for Mr. Hunter. Mr. Hunter was out. When would Mr. Hunter be in?

This cross-talk act was in progress when a little stringy man came up the steps.

"Yes," he said in a thin warble, "What do you want with me? My name is Hunter."

He was dressed in black, with a tall white collar of the sort which always seems to be on the point of cutting the wearer's throat. This was held in place with a thin black rat's tail tie, which disclosed the shiny brass head of the stud.

The Bishop disclosed himself. He didn't sparkle so brightly as the stud.

"Yes, Chief Inspector," the thin voice was puzzled, "What can I do for you?"

"Have you read this morning's papers?" the Chief Inspector asked. "Did you see that Allan Leslie has been murdered? Yes? Well, from his papers it would appear that you dealt with him considerably. I would like to ask you a few questions about him."

"Of course I will do anything I can to help you," Mr. Hunter said, "but I'm afraid that you will find my help of very little use, as I did not know Leslie at all well, and connection was almost entirely a matter of postal communication."

"Is there anywhere here we can talk?" enquired the Bishop, waving a well-manicured plump hand round the dusty entrance to the hall, crowded with dusty palms and pots of Benares brass which looked as though they could do with a polish. His gesture shewed his distaste for the hotel.

Mr. Hunter seemed to think.

"It would probably be as well for us to go out," he announced finally, "there's a tea-shop round the corner where we might find a quiet corner."

"That's fine," Professor Stubbs put in suddenly, "I'm beginnin' to think I could do wi' some moisture. I'm dehydratin' fast."

We adjourned to the A.B.C. in Southampton Row. The Chief Inspector told Hunter the facts about Leslie's death. I watched him closely as the Bishop spoke but he seemed to be genuinely bewildered.

"And," the Chief Inspector went on, "as we were sorting out his papers we came upon evidence which shewed that he was not only the owner of a bookshop in Wesley Street, but that he also had a large postal business as a purveyor of pornographic literature and, we believe was also a dealer in stolen books—not ordinary stolen books, mind you, but really rare stuff—Elizabethan Quartos, incunabula and so on."

"Dear me," Mr. Hunter seemed really shocked, "I would never have suspected him of such activities. He always seemed to me to be the very soul of honour. In all my dealings with him I found him most punctilious and obliging. I never had any cause to complain about any of the books I bought from him. His descriptions of condition were so accurate and so reliable that I could use them myself in quoting a book to a customer. If he said that a book was in fine condition I could rely upon its being in fine condition. When he described a book as having weak joints it had weak joints. I have, of course, heard stories in the trade about his being short tempered and opinionated, but I never encountered anything like that in my connection with him. I never had any cause to cross swords with him, so our relationship was, you might say, almost perfect, a rare thing in the dealings of booksellers with one another, if the relationship is entirely postal."

The Chief Inspector was looking very sleepy. "Just as a matter of routine, Mr. Hunter," he said, "I hope you will not mind telling me where you were yesterday afternoon?"

Mr. Hunter's thin neck seemed to string out from his collar. His little wrinkled face took on a look of outraged virtuousness.

"I'm afraid, Chief Inspector," he said, and his thin voice was as cold as a North Sea breeze among reeds, "that I certainly do object to telling you where I was yesterday afternoon. I was engaged upon business of the utmost confidence and that is all I can tell you. You cannot suspect me of murdering Leslie. I hardly knew the man, and might have passed him in the street without recognising him."

"Ah," the Chief Inspector was smooth, "I'm afraid, Mr. Hunter, that you do not realise the position. It is no more pleasant for me to have to worry you about your private concerns than it is for you to be questioned, but this is a case of murder and I have my duty to do. No doubt your confidential business has nothing to do with the case but you will understand that your refusal to help me makes it very difficult for me to regard you in anything but a suspicious light. I'm afraid that I must ask you again. What were you doing between two and four o'clock yesterday afternoon?"

Mr. Hunter pursed his pale lips.

"I am sorry, Inspector," he said, "but I'm afraid I must be equally firm in telling you that what I was doing yesterday was none of your business. I can assure you that my thoughts were not in the least concerned with Mr. Leslie, and I can also assure you that I did not murder him, but I must insist that I am not in a position to give you any details of my occupation between two and four o'clock yesterday. That the occupation was entirely harmless you may rest assured. You cannot be so stupid as to think that I murdered Mr. Leslie and Mr. Baird, the latter of whom is a stranger to me."

It looked as though a deadlock had been reached. The Chief Inspector seemed to be unwilling to bring out his big guns, but Mr. Hunter seemed to be equally stubbornly decided that he would not help.

The Professor was filling his pipe. When he had at last got it going to his satisfaction he leaned across the table to Mr. Hunter.

"Tell me, son," he rumbled, "if I guess right as to the nature o' yer business, will ye tell me whether I am right?"

Mr. Hunter seemed to be weighing this proposal in his mind. He took a sip, a small ladylike sip, of coffee. Then he nodded.

"Um," the old man was thoughtful, "I'd say ye were engaged in tryin' to estimate the value o' some library, one that's full o' books which ye want, an' ye want to make an offer for the library an' ye want to make dam' certain that no one else in the trade gets wind o' yer deal before it's finished. Perhaps, also, the person whom the books belong to has asked ye to be confidential, maybe they need the money suddenly an' don't want the whole blinkin' world to know o' their need? Maybe ye were called up from Bristol to do the job as that was far enough away to make certain that there'd be no local gossip about the books? Eh, son, am I near the mark?"

Mr. Hunter lit a cigarette carefully. He looked thoughtfully at Professor Stubbs. He seemed to be considering the value of the guess.

"Well, sir," he said thinly, "I don't know what connection you have with the trade. What, none except as a bookbuyer? I couldn't have believed it. Your guess, sir, is correct."

"Um, well, son, don't ye think ye're makin' a bit o' a fool o' yerself by holdin' out on the police. The Chief Inspector here won't go babblin' around town anythin' ye tell him. He's practically as trustworthy as a priest. Anythin' ye tell him that has no connection wi' the case is more or less told him under the seal o' the confessional. If ye're still in doubt, why don't ye phone the person ye're dealing wi', an' get his permission to tell us? Assure him that it'll go no further."

Mr. Hunter thought this over for a moment. He rose to his feet and sorted two pennies from some loose change in his pocket and walked out of the A.B.C. The Chief Inspector shewed some inclination to follow him, but was restrained by the Professor's hand on his arm. Through the large plate glass window he could see Mr. Hunter waiting for the traffic to slow down. He walked across Southampton Row and entered one of the telephone boxes at the corner of Russell Square. We could see him all the time. No one said anything. The

Professor beamed brightly and the Chief Inspector looked sleepily sulky.

Mr. Hunter returned slowly. He sat down with annoying precision. He picked up his cup of coffee which was cold, and ordered another. When that had arrived he took a sip and looked at the Professor.

"Thank you, sir," he said, "your idea was correct. I have my client's permission to use him in support of my, what do you call it, alibi. I was at the house of Mr. Alister Macpherson, at number one hundred and seventy eight Wildgood Grove from eleven o'clock yesterday morning until six o'clock in the evening."

The Chief Inspector grunted unhappily.

Chapter 5

Alibi Absolute

WE HAD eaten well and drunk better and were gathered in the smoking room of the Professor's club. The Chief Inspector who loved good living better than anything else on earth looked somewhat comforted. The glass of brandy beside him glowed dark amber in the dark room and he examined the glowing point of his long cigar with satisfaction.

"As I was saying, John," he said, "and as I'm always saying, the trouble with a murder case is that people cannot think that they are mixed up in it. Surely they cannot be suspected of murdering so-and-so? Therefore they try and make things as difficult as they possibly can be for the police. Look at that silly little man Hunter this morning. All he had to do was give me the address where he had been all afternoon and I could check it up and that would stop my worrying him. However, he must make a shew of secrecy and make things more difficult for us."

"Umhum," the Professor agreed heavily, "ye're right. Murder bein' for the most part the abnormal act o' the normal mind, the ordinary person, whose mind is still workin' along ordinary lines, cannot understand it and resents the fact that he's being dragged into it. Yet, ye see I got a simple mind meself an' I can understand Hunter's unwillin'ness to help ye. It was none o' yer dam' business what he'd been doin' at the time o' the murder. He knew he was not guilty an', if the worst came to the worst he could prove it, so he more or less told ye to go an' boil yer head. I suppose ye're checkin' up on his alibi?"

"Naturally," the Bishop was pontifical, "I have to check every detail. If the Archbishop of Canterbury was connected with a crime and tried to prove that he was holding a service at the time of it, I would still try to find witnesses to make certain he could not have sneaked out through the back and done the deed."

He laughed in a lazy way. I noticed that his eye was fixed on me. It had a fishy quality I did not like.

"Take young Max here," he said, "I know he did not murder Leslie and Baird, but he was around at the time of the murder. I can't swear that he has had no connection with either of the dead men. For all I know he may have been dabbling in the sale of pornography and stolen books. But I know he didn't do the murder. The victims had been dead for some time before he entered the shop, and I have carefully checked up on his movements before then. I have established his alibi from the various shops where he went. He was looking for books that were out of the ordinary, and he is not the sort of person who would pass unnoticed."

I should make it clear that I happen to be abnormally tall and thin and that I have a face that looks as though there had been some prenatal influence from one of the less handsome gargoyles on Notre Dame.

All the same I was mildly irritated to think that the Chief Inspector had gone to the trouble of checking up on my afternoon's pursuits. What the devil would the bookshops think I had been up to? I considered that, as Professor Stubbs's assistant, I should have been considered as the male counterpart of Caesar's wife, and that no suspicion should have been allowed to fall on me.

"Look here," I said, rather hotly, "Do you think I would have rung you up and reported the murder if I'd done it? I was thinking of my pleasant holiday which I have had to postpone. All I wanted to do was to buy a few books and get away as quickly as possible. I hope you made it clear to the assistants and proprietors of the various shops that you were not connecting me with any crime?"

"Of course," the Bishop was suave, "we made it quite clear that it was merely a routine check-up and that there was nothing wrong with either you or your credit. That I think deals with your last question. As for your statement that you wouldn't have rung me up and reported the murder if you had done it. Well, I think that is going just a little bit too far. I don't think you are a fool, Max, but I do think that if you had done the murder you might have thought that, with your connection with the Professor, your action in reporting the crime would have thrown dust in our eyes. That's the sort of thing on which we can take no chances."

I subsided. It was quite true that if I had bumped off Baird and Leslie I might have taken the action the Chief Inspector had outlined.

Before I could think of a reasonable come-back, the aged waiter who had been keeping us supplied with coffee and brandy approached. He leaned over the Chief Inspector.

"You are Chief Inspector Bishop," he said, more as a statement than as a question, "You are wanted on the telephone."

The Chief Inspector carefully removed about three-quarters of an inch of ash from his cigar. He got up and with the heavy grace of a well-fed Persian cat moved silently across the room.

"How d'ye like bein' a suspect, Max?" the old man chortled. "Did ye feel the gates o' the prison-house closin' around ye, eh?"

I treated this remark with the contempt which it deserved.

"That wipes out Hunter," I said coldly, "and myself. There remain to be examined the three others, Read, Hume and Gray. I wonder if we will get any further with them. Have you, with all your cleverness, decided who killed Leslie and Baird? And why they were killed in this way?"

"No," the old man ruffled his grey hair which already looked like a disorderly copse, "I can't say I got many ideas as yet. I want to know a bit more first."

The Chief Inspector strolled back across the room. He lowered himself carefully into the leather covered chair.

"Two little bits of information," he said, "have just come in. The first is that both Baird and Leslie had been knocked out with the proverbial blunt instrument. A blow on the back of the head in both cases. The doctor says that in the case of Leslie, at least, it is doubtful whether he would have lived even if he had not been gassed. The blow caused a serious fracture which would probably have resulted in his death. The other piece of information is that examination of Baird's private papers shews, as I rather suspected, that he was a blackmailer. He seems, from these papers, to have been rather cleverer than most of his unpleasant brethren. The sums that he drew from his victims were comparatively small. Small enough to make the victim think that it was cheaper to pay out than to risk the exposure of a police court. For, as you well know, it's all very well for us to refer in court to Mr. X. The great British public who read their newspapers know nothing at all about Mr. X. But Mr. X. does not care whether the great B.P. knows all about him or not, what he wants to prevent is his own small circle of intimates knowing that Mr. X. is really Mr. John Smith of the Acacias, and that is very much more difficult to manage. As I said, Baird was cunning. He did not bleed his victim dry. He merely asked for a small regular remittance. Drawing, as he did, from a considerable number of victims, this meant that he himself was fairly well-off, while, at the same time, he ran little chance of any of them being so desperate as to risk the publicity. That, of course, is where the professional blackmailer is so difficult to catch. He will not take the risk of killing his golden goose—it is the amateur who wants as much as he can as quickly as possible who drives his victim into desperation and gives us our chance."

"Um," the old man rumbled, "I suppose yer blunt instrument was that shillelagh I saw lyin' in the back-shop yesterday? Eh? It's heavy enough to break a man's skull all right."

"That is possible," the Chief Inspector was weary, "but the trouble there is that a blunt instrument may be anything from the wall of a house to the back of your hand. You know the rabbit-punch in boxing? Yes? Well, that delivered with enough force would apparently break the parts of Leslie that were broken. The doctor told me that when I asked him for an opinion as to what might have caused the damage. Well," he carefully ground out the butt of his cigar, "I suppose I must be getting on with the job. I'm not like you fortunate people who can sit about all afternoon and discuss matters idly as they arise in your minds. I intend to call on Gray, the printseller, whose office is only just around the corner, in St. James's Street."

"Ye don't think ye're goin' wi'out me," the Professor howled, to the intense disgust of several apparently moribund members who took his voice for the Last Trump and sat up abruptly, "Where'd ye get the idea ye can manage this case wi'out me? I'm comin' wi' ye."

He hoisted himself heavily from the chair. It had been a neat fit for him and for a moment I wondered whether it was not going to stick to him like a peculiar snail-shell. It was dislodged from his person just in time. He lumbered across the room after the Chief Inspector. I uncoiled myself regretfully and followed them.

To my relief, the old man decided that he would exercise his limbs to the extent of walking round to Gray's place of business. I looked at the Bentley and shuddered. It seemed to me that the inanimate mass strained at an imaginary leash when it saw its master.

A small notice, written in Eric Gill's *Perpetua* type, informed us that Henry Gray, Prints & Drawings, was on the second floor. We went upstairs, the Professor as he stumped from step to step making a noise like a herd of elephants out on the rampage.

The lettering on the glass door was also carefully executed in *Perpetua*. It looked very tasteful. The girl who opened the door might also have been called tasteful. As far as I was concerned she was a honey. She had dark reddish hair surrounding a clear, pale face.

We asked for Mr. Gray and the Chief Inspector proffered his card. The girl opened the door wider and said quietly, "this is Chief Inspector Bishop, Henry."

We went in. The floor was lushly carpeted. Portfolios stood around on stands and there were various print cabinets with long shallow drawers. The young man who came to meet us was slim and perfectly dressed, in a neat grey Cheviot tweed suit. His hair was perfectly arranged, not one wisp of it out of place. He smiled.

"Ah, yes," he said holding out his hand, "I've been expecting you. Do have a seat."

He gestured towards an Empire couch running down one side of the room. The old man looked at it doubtfully, mentally weighing his bulk against the slender gilt legs. He decided in favour of the risk and lowered himself cautiously on to it. It held. I sat down too. The Chief Inspector did not seem to know what to do, so after a moment's hesitation he followed our example.

Gray seated himself behind a large desk. The girl wafted through wide doors into another half of the room and sat down at a smaller desk covered with papers.

"I suppose," Gray started the ball rolling before the Bishop had time to speak, "that you have come to ask about my connections with the late Mr. Leslie? Yes? Well I supplied him with a considerable amount of material, of all sorts. Some of it, I don't mind admitting, was stuff that I couldn't very well handle myself."

"Uhuh," the old man grunted, "ye sold him dirty drawin's eh? An' he had a market for 'em, while you hadn't, eh? That right, eh?"

Gray turned towards him and bowed slightly.

"You are quite correct in your assumptions," he said, "except for the fact that drawings and prints which I sold him could hardly be included in the category 'dirty drawings.' For the most part they were works by established artists, possessing great artistic merit, but of such a character that, for instance, I could not dispose of them through the ordinary trade channels. For instance there was a painting, supposed to have been by Rubens. I may say that I am quite convinced that it was genuine, but, unfortunately, the subject was not one that could have been placed on the walls of one of our public galleries without causing some considerable comment in the daily press. You may understand, further, that work of this character is not so financially profitable as work that can be generally shewn. I was the possessor of a Rubens, to my mind an indubitable Rubens, for which I should have been able to ask several thousand pounds had it been, shall we say, a little less startling. As it was, however, I was glad to accept Leslie's offer of as many hundred pounds as it was intrinsically worth thousands. I do not deal in these sort of things as a rule, and so I have no channels for disposing of them when they do turn up. Leslie had these channels and so I was glad to cooperate with him. I had paid little for the Rubens and was glad to make a comfortable profit quickly. Had I tried to keep the painting until a customer turned up, it might have stood here for months or even years, and, you will realise that I could not insure it at its true value."

"How did you come to make contact with Leslie in the first place?" the Chief Inspector was bland, "I don't suppose you went around town looking for someone who dealt in a drawing of that nature, did you?"

"Good Lord, no," Gray was amused at the idea of himself totting an obscene Rubens round London under his arm looking for a purchaser, "of course I didn't. I bought a collection of drawings from a runner called Ellis Read. At the time when I bought them he was carrying a portfolio which he undid and shewed to me. The drawings were crude in the extreme. Not at all the sort of thing I would have dealt in myself. Out of idle curiosity I asked him how he hoped to dispose of them, no doubt with a subconscious memory of several eighteenth-century French engravings which I had had lying in a drawer for over a year. He told me that Allan Leslie would always buy such things. I would have dismissed this as of no interest, had not Read gone on to say that, while Leslie bought this trashy dirt, and paid well for it, he was more interested in the irreproducible works that were also works of art. I shewed Read my engravings and he said he would mention them to Leslie. I forgot all about until a week later when Leslie suddenly appeared here. He gave me a very good price for the engravings, so after that, should such material turn up, I always communicated with him. I must say on his behalf, that the prices which he gave were usually within a few pounds of what I could have obtained for them myself, and there was the added advantage that there was no delay in turning them into money."

The Chief Inspector digested this information slowly. The old man was engaged in the business of lighting his pipe.

"Just as a matter of routine, Mr. Gray," the Bishop's formula flowed easily from his tongue, "I wonder if you would mind telling me what you were doing yesterday afternoon?"

Gray did not seem to be the least perturbed.

"If you want my alibi," he said cheerfully, "the trouble is that I haven't got one. Not the veriest shadow of an alibi. All I can say is that I didn't murder Leslie, for he was very useful to me when he was alive."

"What do you mean?" the Chief Inspector looked very weary.

"You see," Gray was ingenuous, "I was going to visit Leslie yesterday afternoon. I have six obscene drawings by Henry Fuseli, the eighteenth century Anglo-Swiss artist, and I thought I would take them round to him. When I looked into his shop I could see, through the open door of the back room, that he was talking to someone, so I went away. To fill in the time I went to a news cinema. When I returned, I saw a bobby standing in the door of the shop, and, considering the nature of the drawings in the small portfolio under my arm, I thought that discretion was the better part of curiosity and buzzed off back here."

Chapter 6

That's My Business

THE PROFESSOR was humming softly to himself. It sounded like the distant rumbling of an underground train. The tune was *Oh who will o'er the hills with me*. The Chief Inspector pulled at his lower lip, with his plump finger and thumb.

"That is unfortunate, Mr. Gray," he said in a listless voice, "I suppose, however, that we may find that someone remembers sitting next to you in the news-reel?"

"No, you won't," Gray was still cheerful, "I had a row practically to myself, and I'm quite sure that the girl at the cash-desk didn't notice me. She was reading *Peg's Paper* or something of the sort and didn't look up when I plunked down my bob. I've been over the whole thing myself several times and, so far as I can see, I haven't even the merest ghost of an alibi. Now what do you do? Arrest me?"

"I hardly think the situation calls for that, Mr. Gray," the Chief Inspector was ponderous, "but it is a pity that I cannot clear you out of the way. I suppose you can give me a rough idea of the time you went out?"

"Mary," Gray called to the girl who came in. "This is my wife," he introduced her and went on, "I seem to have landed myself in a bit of soup. What time did I start out to go and see old Leslie, dear?"

Mary Gray wrinkled her brow. I thought she looked even nicer when she looked worried. Judging from her looks alone I'd have said Gray was a damned lucky man.

"We went out early for lunch," she said slowly, "and I suppose we finished about half-past one to a quarter to two. Then we came back here and you picked up the Fuselis, saying you would run round to old Leslie with them. I suppose you left here a little before two, dear. The people in the restaurant may be able to fix it more accurately than I can, as they were quite obviously waiting for the table we were using."

"Um, son," the old man was gentle, "I thought ye said that Leslie usually came round to see you. Why the flamin' hurry to rush round to him?"

"As a matter of fact, sir," Gray was not perturbed, "I have been offered rather a fine collection of English Romantic drawings. You know the kind of thing—there is a pencil and wash drawing which *might* be by Blake, an early Samuel Palmer, a landscape by James Ward, several drawings—printable ones this time—by Fuseli, a rather good little water-colour by Stothard, and so on. The price of the collection is rather high, and I wanted to draw in as much cash as I possibly can, as quickly as possible, in order to cover myself on the purchase. You see, I know the collection is worth at least five times what I am being asked for it, but it happens that I wasn't expecting to have to lay out several hundred pounds at the moment. I recently bought a very fine collection of Rembrandt etchings and that has set me back a bit. The obscene Fuselis are worth about a hundred and twenty and that would have helped. As a matter of fact," his voice was thoughtful, "the murder of old Leslie has put me in a bit of a hole. I'll have to raise that money in some other way."

"I'll lend it to ye, son," the Professor was suddenly surprisingly generous. He dug through the mass of papers in his jacket pocket and finally located a rather moth-eaten cheque-book. He borrowed my fountain pen and wrote a cheque, payable to Henry Gray, for a hundred and fifty pounds.

The Bishop sat there looking as if someone was pulling his hair.

"I say, sir," Gray was genuinely embarrassed, "that's most awfully decent of you. I don't know that I can let you do it, though. I mean I may be run in on a charge of bumping off old Leslie and then where will your money be?"

"Ye can leave that to me," the old man gave a villanous wink in the direction of Mary Gray who accepted it as if he had smiled a beaming and benevolent smile.

Gray was looking at the signature on the cheque. I suddenly realised that we had not been introduced to him, and that it must be a bit startling when a large middle-aged gentleman, looking rather like a half-grown elephant, suddenly lands in your office and starts doling out cheques.

"Good Lord," Gray was astonished, "I know who you are sir. I remember your work on the murder of Arthur Trelawny. He had bought one or two things from me and so, naturally, I was interested in the case. Besides I know Ambrose Gopher. Did you know that he had married Sybil Montague?"

The Chief Inspector's face said more plainly than words could that he had not come to Gray's office to indulge in social gossip. Mary Gray coughed gently and her husband looked round at the Bishop.

"I am sorry, Chief Inspector," he said, "I forgot that you are here on business. I don't think that I can do anything to help you, except ask you to believe me when I say that the thought of murdering Leslie was as far from my mind as the thought of buying a genuine Leonardo. I seem to be rather awkwardly placed, not having an alibi, but I didn't murder Leslie."

"I'd ha' bin much more willin' to consider ye as murderer," the old man broke in, "if ye'd had a perfect alibi. What I'd like to ask ye is what ye know o' Leslie apart from yer business dealin's wi' him."

"Damn little," Gray was frank, "I didn't have anything to do with him except as a method of disposing of difficult works. As I've said he usually came round here. I don't suppose I've been in his shop half-a-dozen times in my life. He just used to come round here when I dropped him a note that I had something that might interest him. He would look at the drawing, ask me what I wanted for it and write me a cheque. He never haggled over the price. I have heard that he disliked the business of beating a man down on his price, and I was always careful to ask him what seemed to me a reasonable price. If I was not sure what something was worth, he would make me an offer for it, and it was always an offer that I accepted with gratitude. Oh, yes. Once when he came he was accompanied by a lady whom he introduced as his niece, a Miss—now what was it?—ah, yes, Wright. Extraordinary old bird she was. With a hat like a haystack, an ostrich feather boa, and an umbrella with an enormous nobbly head clutched to her bosom. She impressed me as belonging to a date earlier than her uncle's birth. You see, I'm sorry but that is all I know about his private life."

The Chief Inspector rose to his feet.

"Well, Mr. Gray," his tone was official, "I'm sorry we have had to take up your time like this. I hope you will understand that I have no option but to ask you to remain available should we wish to call on you further. I would be grateful if you would try and see if you can remember seeing anyone on your outing yesterday afternoon who might remember you. If you could it would be a great help."

Gray shook his head doubtfully. It was obvious that he had no hope that he would be able to establish an alibi.

Someone knocked on the door. Mary Gray walked across and opened it. She turned to her husband.

"It's Mr. Read," she said, "with one or two drawings which he thinks might interest you."

Before Gray could reply, the Chief Inspector spoke. "Mr. Ellis Read?" he asked. Mary Gray nodded, "Have him in. I wanted to see him."

A small round man appeared in the room. His round head was as innocent of hairs as a billiard ball. His cheeks were rosy and his little stub-nose was red.

"Good afternoon, Mr. Gray," he began, and then he noticed us. He waited for someone to say something. The Chief Inspector came forward, rather like a schoolboy being pushed forward by his fellows to perform some unpleasant duty.

"Mr. Read?" he asked again, and the little round head nodded briskly. "Mr. Read, I am Chief Inspector Bishop and I am investigating the deaths of Mr. Allan Leslie and Mr. Cecil Baird. I believe you were closely associated with Mr. Leslie? That's right, isn't it?"

"Why lord bless you, sir," Read was as cheerful and unperturbed as Gray, "I'm closely associated, as you say, with half the booksellers and picture dealers in town. They want something and they ask me and I find it. That's my business. You want a drawing by Constable—well I'll find you one. You want a copy of the *Lyrical Ballads*—I'll find it for you. That's my business."

"Precisely," the Chief Inspector interrupted the flow. "I believe that, among the things which you used to find for Mr. Leslie were indecent drawings and books? That's right?"

Read was unembarrassed.

"Of course I found them for him," he said, "it's none of my business what he did with them when I got them for him. I don't pretend to look after other people's morals. Mr. Leslie wanted obscene drawings and pornographic books, I found them for him. That's my business. Mr. Gray here wants good English drawings and good prints. I find them for him. That's my business."

It occurred to me that neither Gray nor Ellis had shewn any fear of the law relating to the sale of obscene productions.

"As you probably know," the Chief Inspector said, rather stiffly, "both you and Mr. Gray here have been guilty of a crime in dealing with these drawings. I do not propose myself to do anything about it. The matter of public morals does not lie within my sphere. But I feel

I should remind you that you have committed punishable offences, and that, quite apart from all considerations dealing with the murders, you are liable to suffer a criminal prosecution."

"Lord bless you, sir," Read was amused, "I know that. But have you thought how difficult it would be to prosecute either of us for selling the work of a man who is reputed to be a master. I'd like to hear the prosecution presenting a case accusing me of handling an obscene Rubens. Why, lord bless you, sir, if such a case came into court we could call every art expert in the country, from the Director of the National Gallery down, to prove that the work was a work of art primarily and a bit of obscenity second. Why, sir, you'd be laughed out of court. I know that you can deal in any dirt, sir, so long as it is attached to a reputable name, sir. I know. That's my business."

The Chief Inspector seemed a bit put out by this line of attack. I realised that Read was quite correct in his assumption. It would have been a difficult case to bring into court. However the Bishop was indomitable. He returned to the attack.

"I don't wish to know about the drawings by great masters which you sold, Mr. Read," he said. "What I would like to know about is the other stuff you sold Leslie—the stuff that was just plain dirt and nothing else?"

Read's face took on a look of the greatest virtue. He appeared deeply shocked by the Chief Inspector's suggestion that he might handle simple pornography.

"Why, bless you, sir," he said, "I don't handle that kind of stuff at all. Ask anyone in the trade and they'll tell you that I am very careful about the stuff I handle. When I produce a drawing as by an artist, it is by that artist. That's my business. This afternoon I have brought Mr. Gray a bundle of drawings. Six are by John Martin and there is one by Hogarth. The Martin's are all right. I know. But Hogarth's drawings are rare. I say this is a Hogarth. I know I am right. That's my business."

He whipped a tattered portfolio on to Gray's desk, undid a piece of twine and opened it. He spread the drawings out over the surface of the desk.

"Look at that now," he said proudly, choosing a drawing, "Give me your frank opinion. I say it's by Hogarth and I ought to know," and passing it to Gray. "Is that by Hogarth or is it not? Give me an honest opinion. I like to know. That's my business."

Read's refrain about things being his business was beginning to get on my nerves. Every time he opened his mouth I found I was waiting for it. It was like the dropping of water from a leaking tap—if it had not come I would have been more irritated.

Gray picked up the drawing carefully. He looked at it and moved over to the window to get a better light. He turned it this way and that and took a magnifying glass out of his pocket. He examined it in this way for a couple of minutes, during which we sat in silence. He came back to his desk and laid the drawing down.

"Yes, Read," he said pleasantly, "I think there is no doubt about it. I'll buy it from you as a Hogarth."

"Lord bless you," Read turned to us, "you see I'm right. I knew I was right. That's my business. When I say a drawing is by any artist you can bet your boots it is by that artist. Ask anyone in the trade and they'll tell you I'm mostly right. That's my business."

We seemed to be wandering away from the subject we had started with. The Chief Inspector looked as miserable and weary as a Dalmation hound that had run twenty miles behind a carriage. He sighed heavily.

"Yes, Mr. Read," his voice was full of restrained tiredness, "I am ready to allow that you are an expert on your subjects, but I did not ask you about your qualifications as a finder of drawings. What I want to know is your connection with Leslie? Your name appears very frequently as one to whom he paid various sums of money. What were these sums for?"

"Bless you," Read was imperturbable, "Mr. Leslie was a bookseller and he was always asking me to find certain books for him. Say one of his clients wanted a first edition of Locke's *Essay on Human Understanding* or a novel published during the war and out of print. Why, the next time he saw me, Mr. Leslie would ask me to find it. I would find it. That's my business. It's no good you thinking that I kept Mr. Leslie supplied with pornography, for I only sold him what I came across in the way of business. I was glad to have a good market for it, so I passed it on to him, but I didn't go out of my way to find it."

"Yes," the Chief Inspector was very quiet, "and who supplied Mr. Leslie with the stolen books in which he also dealt?"

Read was indignant.

"You can ask anyone in the trade and they'll swear to my honesty," he said hotly. "Why, bless you, sir, do you think I'd last ten days if word got around that I wasn't honest? I am very careful about what I buy. I run no risks of handling stolen goods. Honesty's my policy, and I don't want to spoil it by damaging my reputation. Why, sir, you ask

Mr. Gray here if he's ever heard anyone say anything about my being dishonest. No one ever has, have they, Mr. Gray?"

Gray supported Read's statement. His reputation was absolutely untarnished.

"Thank you, Mr. Gray," the Bishop said wearily. "Now Mr. Read, just as a matter of routine I wonder whether you would mind telling me where you were yesterday afternoon?"

"Why, bless you, sir," the little round head nodded, "I was in my cellar in Marchmont Street, where I keep the bulk of my things. I was colouring a copy of Thomas Shotter Boys's *London*. I have a client who wants a coloured copy. I've told him that it was never issued coloured, but he insists on having one. So I'm colouring it for him. That's my business."

Chapter 7

Silent Suspect

THE CHIEF INSPECTOR looked as weary as if he had all the cares of the world sitting on his shoulders. He looked at Read lazily.

"I suppose, Mr. Read," his voice was listless, "there is someone who can prove that you were in your cellar? Someone saw you going in or coming out? Perhaps you bought a newspaper, or spoke to someone?"

"Bless you, no, sir. I just go there when I feel like it, and I don't speak to anyone in the district. I keep my drawings and prints and books there. If anything out of the ordinary comes my way, I buy it. That's my business. Sooner or later someone will want it, and I'll make my profit on it."

The old man just sat there, like a caricature of G. K. Chesterton trying to look like Buddha. The foul smoke from his short pipe wreathed him like wisps of incense smoke. He looked as benevolent as a baby elephant who has not yet discovered its strength.

"Dammit," the Chief Inspector was peevish, "why is it my luck to run into cases where everyone has a perfect alibi or where no one has any alibi at all? If either you, Mr. Gray, or you, Mr. Read, should happen to remember anything that will help me, or help shew where you were in the afternoon, I hope you will get in touch with me at the Yard."

He rose to his feet and scowled at Professor Stubbs who was still full of silence. The old man hoisted himself upright too, and I uncoiled myself and prepared to follow them.

At the door the old man turned.

"Mr. Gray," he said politely, "I'll be pleased if ye an' yer wife," his gesture might have passed as a bow, "will consider takin' a bite o' dinner wi' me to-morrow night. Here's me card."

From one of his waistcoat pockets he dug a dirty slip of ivory cardboard which he handed over with a polite gesture. He always carried cards like that. They were not very nice cards as they had been printed for him by a friend of his, a small jobbing printer who had no range of types. When I was a kid I had been told by one of my more snobbish uncles that a gentleman, meaning the sort of fellow he considered himself to be, always had engraved cards. It is the sort of memory that sticks in one's mind, like walking on the outside of the pavement when accompanying a lady. The old man's cards were printed in a very florid nineteenth century Gothic type and made no pretence to being engraved.

Mrs. Gray said that she and her husband would be delighted to have dinner with Professor Stubbs and we lumbered down the stairs and out into the cool afternoon light of St. James's Street.

I walked behind the Professor and the Chief Inspector as we went back to collect the car.

"Where're ye goin' now," the old man said, "as I'm comin' wi' ye? Ye've still got another man to see, ain't ye? Where's he hang out?"

"Oh, yes," the Bishop was not encouraging, "there is still Charles Hume. He has a small shop in Fulham. I suppose we might as well call on him and see what he has to say for himself. I've been more or less keeping him to the last, as he is my most likely suspect. I have heard that, although he has never been caught, his reputation is inclined to be shady and he is supposed to be a fence for stolen books and pictures. As you know, we have various specialists at the Yard, and one of them, who is an authority on the thieves who go in for the *object d'art* which cannot be sold through the usual channels, said that he had his eye on Hume for some time. You can come along with me if you like."

His tone was ungracious and damping, but it did not impress the old man. He grinned at the unhappy Chief Inspector.

"I'll drive ye down," he announced, "that'll blow the depression out o' yer head."

The Bishop shuddered, but apparently felt that he had nothing to live for anyhow and climbed into the Bentley. The journey passed without incident. We managed to negotiate Hyde Park Corner and finally found ourselves in the King's Road.

Out beyond the World's End we turned up a narrow street and drew up outside a small bookshop. The owner of the shop apparently was also interested in engravings as the sides of the windows were hung with odds and ends, ranging from a framed soft-ground etching of one of the Normandy castles by John Sell Cotman to a parrot from Edward

Lear's great book on the parrots. We opened the glass door of the shop.
A tinny bell jangled.

Mr. Hume was apparently not interested in customers. He kept us
waiting for a few minutes. Then, up a stair-case at the back of the shop,
half-hidden by piles of books and framed engravings a large round head
appeared, topped by a black tight-fitting skull-cap. This was followed
by a large flabby man, who grunted at the exertion of climbing the
stairs.

He looked at us out of eyes that seemed strangely disconcerting.
They were like small blue pebbles in a pink sea. I suddenly realised that
the thing which gave them their terrifying quality was that there was
no hair surrounding them. The face of Mr. Hume was hairless. Not an
eyebrow, eyelash or whisker disturbed its smoothness.

"Yes?" he stood expectantly at the head of the stairs, resting his hand
upon a pile of books while he recovered his breath. "What can I do for
you?"

The Chief Inspector moved forward.

"Mr. Hume? Yes? I am Chief Inspector Bishop. I am investigating
the murders of Mr. Allan Leslie and Mr. Cecil Baird. It appears from
Mr. Leslie's papers that you were connected with him in business. Is
this correct?"

"Yes," said Mr. Charles Hume. We waited for him to go on, but he
apparently was one of those who believed in saving his breath.

"What," the Chief Inspector tried again, "were your relations with
him?"

"Business," said Mr. Hume briefly.

"What kind of business?" the Bishop shewed no signs of the irritation which I knew was creeping up in him like a flowing tide.

"Bookselling," said Mr. Hume.

"Dammit, son," the old man was not so patient as the Chief
Inspector, "we didn't think ye were in the habit o' sellin' him chunks
off the moon, or even fish or meat. We know ye're a bookseller an'
he's another. What would ye be dealin' in if not in books?"

"I sometimes sold him books and sometimes he sold them to me,"
Mr. Hume seemed positively garrulous by comparison.

"Yes?" the Chief Inspector seemed to be waiting, but having made
his statement Mr. Hume seemed to be saving his breath. I started to
look around the shop. I spied a beautiful copy of the coloured engraving of *The Night-Blowing Cereus* from Dr. John Robert Thornton's

Sexual System of Plants. I thought I would buy it if it was not too deadly. Mr. Hume did not seem to be in a talkative mood.

"That is all?" he enquired politely, and turned to go downstairs again. The Chief Inspector was as angry as a turkey cock, but it did not shew in his face.

"I'm afraid not, Mr. Hume," his voice was as cold as charity, "I must ask you to give me an account of your movements yesterday afternoon?"

"I was here," Mr. Hume replied and waited for the Chief Inspector to proceed.

"Have you any proof you were here?"

"No."

"Were there any customers in your shop ?"

"Several," Hume was not interested. Getting replies out of him seemed to be like drawing the teeth of a shark. There was always another tooth, but there did not seem to be any future in the job.

"Will any of these customers state that they bought a book from you?" The Chief Inspector was slowly becoming exasperated.

"No."

"Why not? Surely you know who some of them are?"

"I sold no books. People looked round and went away."

The Chief Inspector shrugged his shoulders. Mentally I could see he was passing the ball to the Professor, who took it cheerfully and tried to score.

"Ye're not what ye might call communicative, son," he grumbled, "If ye were to use a bit more breath it might save us all a bit o' time. Can't ye give us an account o' how ye spent the afternoon an' a bit clearer idea o' yer connections wi' Leslie."

"No," Mr. Hume was still polite, but his voice was firm. His little eyes were watching me, without interest, as I fished among the books. The stock was not outstanding. I could see nothing that I wanted and my tastes are fairly catholic.

"I may say, Mr. Hume," the Chief Inspector had rallied, "that your attitude is not calculated to do you any good. I must ask you to remain available for further questioning."

"Yes," Charles Hume was bored. He turned to retreat down the stairs.

"How much is this?" I asked, waving *The Night-Blowing Cereus.*

"Two pounds ten," he replied. The price was ridiculous. I pulled out the money and gave it to him. He pushed the notes into his trouser-pocket and turned his back on us, going puffing down the stairs.

I thought the old man was about to blow up. There was the sort of repressed snorting which one associates with active volcanoes going on beside me. I turned to look at him. I then realised that he was laughing at the Chief Inspector who was ignoring him, pointedly.

We left the shop and climbed back into the car. I clutched my engraving to me.

"Huh," the old man was jubilant, "that got ye, Reggie. Ye'll squeeze milk out o' a stone as soon as get a story out o' Mr. Hume. He didn't seem to like ye?"

"No," the Bishop had recovered his equanimity and was again as bland as butter. "However, we'll see whether Mr. Hume continues to be able to behave in this manner. I don't mind if he likes me or not, but he cannot be permitted to treat the police in this manner. I'll have him pulled in for questioning tomorrow morning."

"Uhhuh," the Professor nodded wisely, "he's the sort o' feller that must make ye wish ye had the powers o' yer American colleagues, eh? I'll bet ye'd like to beat some words out o' him wi' a bit o' hose pipe?"

"No," the Chief Inspector was thoughtful. "I doubt whether the American police, with all their third-degree, can get ahead much faster than we can. After all, if Barclay is right and Hume is a sort of fence, you can understand his unwillingness to talk to us. He would also know that, so long as he did not wilfully interfere with the police in the execution of their duty, there was no reason for him to do more than answer our questions. And you must admit, John, that he *did* answer our questions. He did exactly all that we asked of him. I did not wish to draw in the question of the stolen books at the moment, but want him to think he is fairly safe from our interference, except so far as it concerns Leslie. He'll probably have a good story worked out for us by tomorrow morning, when I'll get him to come in for some more questions. It will be absolutely watertight and absolutely untrue. However, it will give us something to work on, and we'll see how Mr. Hume likes that."

The Professor started the car. Once we were travelling all ordinary conversation became an impossibility. This was unfortunate as a little light conversation might have helped distract the too painful attention of the passengers from the road and the less than hair-breadth escapes.

We pulled up at the Professor's club and were soon surrounded by tea and hot-buttered muffins.

Suddenly I had a bright idea.

"I say," I said to the Bishop, "can you find out what rare and out of the ordinary books have been stolen recently? If you could find that out, now that Leslie is dead you might be able to connect them with Hume, if he really is a fence. If you can get enough evidence together, maybe you could apply for a search warrant and you might then find the books in his possession."

The Chief Inspector did not seem to be very impressed with this idea, but I was insistent and finally he rose to his feet.

"All right, Max," he said, "if you really think it will help you any, I'll go and ring Barclay and ask him."

He was only away for two or three minutes. When he came back he handed me a slip of paper.

"Here's your list," he said, "and I hope it'll do you a lot of good."

There were four books on the list. *The Book of Thel* by William Blake, a copy not mentioned in Geoffrey Keynes's *Bibliography*, and worth about seven hundred pounds; *An Anatomy of the World* by John Donne, 1611; a presentation copy from the author of Donne's *Pseudo-Martyr*, 1610; and a presentation copy of John Evelyn's *Sculptura*, 1662, given to Robert Hooke, the ingenious microscopist.

I looked at the list and whistled softly. There was no doubt that the book-thief who had stolen these things knew what he was after and must also have some way of disposing of them. There was not one of these items which could have been sold over the counter in even the most expensive West End bookshop without a pedigree. Anyone who bought such items would need to keep them to himself, for they were all things that any book collector would have given almost anything to possess.

"Good Lord," I said, "don't you realise that if you find one of these items in Hume's possession you've got him well and proper?"

"I don't see that," the Bishop was mildly obtuse, "one book is very like another book. Certainly the thief could remove the presentation inscriptions from the books that have it, but then I could not prove that the book was not his own all the time."

The old man leaned over and took the list from me. Even he pursed up his lips and grunted.

"Harumph, Reggie," he snorted suddenly, "there's probably a dozen men in this country who could describe every detail of these books to you from memory. They'd be able to tell ye all the pages which are a trifle short an' also whether there was a damp stain on any o' 'em. If ye can find any o' these books I'm willing to bet ye'll find the answer to the book-stealin'. When it looked as though Leslie was dealin' in stolen books, I never dreamed he was flyin' as high as this. If ye'd that little bundle in yer hand, an' could sell it wi' an honest pedigree, in an ordinary auction, ye'd be able to retire from the police-force for a year or two, livin' on the proceeds wi' more comfort than ye draw from yer present salary."

The Chief Inspector negotiated a drop of melted butter with his pink tongue. He did not seem to be impressed.

"All I can say is that there are a lot of fools in the world," he announced cheerfully, "just imagine giving all that money for a handful of books. Cor!"

Chapter 8

Books within Books

I GAVE it up. There is no point in fracturing one's toenails by kicking against a granite wall. And I might just as well have told myself from the start that the old man would have his way. He always does.

After I had done my morning chores, going round and inspecting the plants for the slightest traces of mildew or other sickness, I agreed quite meekly when, at breakfast, Professor Stubbs drew his tartan dressing gown around him like a martial cloak.

"What d'ye say to goin' visitin' again this mornin'?" he asked. "I was thinkin' it might be a good idea to go an' see Miss Wright an' see if she can tell us anythin' about her brother."

"All right," I was not enthusiastic, but resigned, "I'll come with you. At the same time, I think I should remind you that you are a botanist and not a member of the police-force and that we are wasting the hell of a lot of time on things that don't concern us."

"Don't concern us, eh?" the Professor was noisily indignant. "Here's me assistant goes stumblin' into corpses an' he wants to say it's none o' our business. What, I'd ask ye, do ye consider to be our business?"

He appealed to an invisible choir of angels who apparently gave him great moral support. I looked at the black dregs in my coffee cup. If the old man had been a donkey I might have tried to argue his hind-leg off, but as things were he was impregnable.

The Professor drove the old Bentley with an air of great abstraction. This would have been all right, if he could have kept his subconscious mind on the road, but he didn't. By the time we reached Streatham I felt that my hair was permanently on end. Trams are the devil.

The house was one of a row of small late Victorian houses, possessing an air of decayed gentility, faintly reminiscent of those shops where distressed gentlewomen sell the most appalling objects, made from indescribably hairy wool and sealing wax.

Miss Wright opened the door to us herself.

"Oh, good morning," she said, "I do hope you will pardon the mess. My maid left without notice last night and has left me in this state of chaos."

The house was as tidy as the Professor's was not. Brass objects shone yellow in the morning sun, dust was a stranger to the house and white linen antimacassars covered the backs of the tapestried armchairs where we seated ourselves. I looked for the aspidistra. Sure enough it was there, sitting on a bamboo what-not near the window. There was also a castor-oil plant and a juniper. Come the winter I could have betted on the azaleas, flame and white, in pots hidden in larger pots of tasteful green glaze and Benares brass from Birmingham.

"Humph," the Professor seated himself heavily, "I hope ye'll pardon the intrusion, ma'am? I was wonderin' if ye'd tell us a few facts about yer uncle."

"Isn't it dreadful," Miss Wright was pained, "the police say that he was a criminal. I would never have dreamed that Uncle Allan could have done all the things they say he did. He was always so upright and so punctilious in all his dealings. They say he dealt in stolen books. I'm sure it must all be a terrible mistake. He would never have done that. They were here yesterday and they took away all his private papers. It's terrible. I don't know what the neighbours can be saying."

Professor Stubbs was sympathetic. He leaned forward as he spoke in a surprisingly gentle voice.

"I'm sure, ma'am," he said, "that the police were as unofficious as they possibly can be. I was wonderin' if ye'd mind tellin' us what yer uncle was like to live wi'?"

"Of course, I'll be only too glad to help you find out who did this terrible thing. Uncle Allan and I got on very well together. He was not altogether easy to live with, as he resented anything which might be called interference. Why, I remember one day when I started to dust his books he was most terribly angry. He said that when he wanted them fiddled with he would ask me, but until then he would thank me not to touch his things. But I must say that he was reasonable. He knew how much I hated anything like dust and after that he would borrow a feather duster from me and deal with the books himself."

"Um, ma'am," the old man was thoughtful, "I wonder if ye'd mind just shewin' us yer uncle's room. Ye know," he sounded vague, "it's sometimes helpful to see a man's room. Kinda gives ye a picture o' his mind an' some indication o' the sort o' feller he was an' so on."

"Not the least."

Miss Wright rose briskly to her feet, the silver chains of the chatelaine she affected jangling cheerfully. I noticed that among the incongruous objects she carried thus suspended from her waist were a silver candle-snuffer and a silver-covered bottle of smelling salts. It looked to me as though the old bird went around prepared for all eventualities.

Professor Stubbs hoisted himself wheezingly out of the chair where he had been ensconced like a philosophic bullfrog. We followed Miss Wright up the stairs, to the gentle tinkling of her accoutrements.

She opened a door on the first floor and we went in. The walls were covered to a height of about six feet with bookshelves; above these there hung some pretty bad oil-paintings. Miss Wright saw me looking at these.

"Family portraits," she said with a quick birdlike motion of her hand, "Some of them are supposed to be very good. Look at this one. It is by Sir Francis Grant. You know he was President of the Royal Academy?"

I nodded politely. The painting was appalling. The subject was a young woman who looked like a washed-out ghost of one of Sir Thomas Lawrence's sitters, and the painting seemed to have been done by the ghost of that painter, after a pretty stiff half-century in hell.

The old man, as was his habit, wandered round the bookshelves, peering at the contents through his steel-rimmed glasses. So far as I could see the books were mostly sets of the English authors, all of them bound in calf. I noticed one or two early editions of Jane Austen. They were in very pretty contemporary binding, but, of course the binder had chopped the edges. There was nothing on the shelves which could possibly be stolen property, at least of the sort and standard with which Leslie had dealt.

"Harrumph," the Professor snorted like a small elephant; I jumped but Miss Wright was not disturbed. "Ma'am, 'ud ye mind shewin' me which books it was that yer uncle picked on ye for dustin'?"

Miss Wright seemed a trifle surprised by this request, but creased her brows in thought.

"I'm not sure that I can remember," she said slowly, "but I think it was these big ones along the bottom."

She gave a quick flick of her hand in the direction of a row of large quarto volumes, bound in red morocco with a lot of gilding. I stooped down and looked at them. They were volumes of *The Art Journal*, dating from the 1870's on. I wondered what on earth had made Leslie want to keep them. They occupied an intolerable amount of shelf-space, and could not possibly have been of any interest to anyone except a student of English painting during the second half of the nineteenth century. Even such students of the subject as I knew baulked at the prospect of filling their houses with the immense tomes, and contented themselves with consulting the volumes in the libraries of the British Museum or the Victoria and Albert.

With considerable difficulty, for he was not built for such things, the old man bent down and examined the backs of the books. He straightened up, puffing like an aged steam-engine.

"Oi you, Max," he rumbled at me, "Ye'd better take a look at these books. Ye're younger than I am an' bendin' don't seem to incommode ye to the same extent. Look through 'em all an' see if there's anythin' odd about 'em. Open every page."

I did not know what Professor Stubbs was up to. However, I was obedient and I lowered my lanky length towards the floor and pulled out the first volume.

I learned more about the appearance of Victorian furniture than I would have believed possible. I read the obituaries of painters who are not only dead but forgotten by all save the compilers of dictionaries. I learned a bit about the progress of photography, but it was not until I had looked through six volumes that I found anything of any interest.

All this time the Professor sat on the edge of a chair grunting to himself. Out of respect for Miss Wright's house he had asked for permission to smoke and had refrained from lighting his filthy little pipe; instead he smoked a Burma cheroot which smelt just as bad. Miss Wright excused herself, with the remark that perhaps we would like a cup of tea, of China tea. This went to the old man's heart as it was one of his theories that he dehydrated very quickly, and the immense drafts of coffee he had engulfed at breakfast had already dried up.

I was half way through the seventh volume when I found that the pages refused to turn. They were stuck together for a thickness of over an inch. I tried to open them in vain. The old man leaned forward with a look of interest.

"Give it here, son," he said, and I handed the volume to him. He looked at it carefully, running his blunt fingers delicately round the bright gilt edges. Then he looked at the back of the binding, where it was sewn with a strip of hard silk at the top. He pulled at this silk gently and the stuck-up portion of the book came away in his hand. It slid out as if in a groove. He passed the portion over to me, after glancing at it. I saw that it was a box. It was empty.

After that I had better luck. The next six volumes were also boxes. Out of them I got one or two finds; several mildly indecent French eighteenth century engravings and some quite good modern obscene drawings mixed up with some of the terrible Japanese productions which are prepared for the tourist trade and some horrible photographs whose home seemed to be somewhere in the eastern Mediterranean.

The next volume was an ordinary one. I examined the rococco brasswork on machinery but found nothing out of the ordinary. It was in the next volume, three from the end, that I made my find.

I pulled at the silk and the back slid away in my hand. I tilted the box into my open hand and a small book, bound in black calf with an orange red leather label slipped out.

I handled this carefully and read the title: *EVELYN'S SCULPTURA*. I opened the book carefully at the title. It was the first edition all right, with the mezzo-tint by Prince Rupert. As clean as the day it was printed, the book was a lovely copy, but that was not the most important thing about it. On the fly-leaf there was a note which ran, "For my honor'd Friend, Dr. Hooke. From his most humble Servant J. Evelyn."

I could hardly forbear a cry of triumph as I passed the book over to the old man. He took it as carefully as if it had been made of egg-shell china.

"Huh," he grunted, "you got somethin' there, Max. I think we got one up on the coppers, eh?"

He chuckled wickedly to himself and held out his hand for the case from which it had come. I passed it over. He held the case up to the light and squinted into it. Folded across the bottom lay a half sheet of note-paper. The weight of the *Sculptura* had pressed it down so that it lay gently fixed. The Professor inserted a finger and pulled it out.

He opened the paper with annoying deliberation. On it was scrawled one word in Leslie's untidy hand. That word was "Hume."

"Hullo," I said, "it's even better than we could have hoped for, isn't it? Here we have the link between Leslie and Hume and a stolen book. This'll make him whistle all right, won't it?"

The old man shook his head slowly. His mop of grey hair wagged as his head moved. He pursed his lips together and then blew heavily.

"No," his voice was deep and rumbling, "I'm afraid that we haven't got anything much here. Just ye put yerself in Hume's position an' see what ye'd do. Why, son, ye'd claim that Leslie had got hold o' the stolen book an' was goin' to try to palm it off on you. Ye'd say o' course ye'd ha' had yer doubts about it, but comin' from an apparently unimpeachable source like the late Mr. Leslie ye'd not bother much an' would ha' bought it. Mind you, son, it was not till Leslie was killed that we found out that he was a dealer in dirty an' stolen books. While he was alive he might ha' passed as a pillar o' the established church. I've no doubt that he was looked upon as a most respectable feller, payin' his debts punctually an' never gettin' drunk. Come to think o't," his voice was reflective, "they'll be openin' soon an' we who are not respectable members o' society an' who ha' no reputations to lose can go an' get a drink."

The thought cheered him. I slipped the copy of *Sculputura* back into the case along with the piece of paper and replaced it in the binding and back on the shelves. In one of the remaining volumes, the only one that was a box, I found an unbound pamphlet, *Jacob's Vow a Sermon* by Thomas Fuller, 1644. This I discovered later was one of the rarest of Thomas Fuller's books, only two copies being recorded in the bibliography of him; undoubtedly Leslie had been in touch with some pretty expert thieves. The funny thing that transpired about this pamphlet was that no one claimed it and so legally it belonged to Leslie's estate. No one had the least doubt that it was a stolen book, but the only explanation that we could think of was that it had been tied up loosely in a bundle of pamphlets in some library which had not been catalogued and that someone employed there, possibly to catalogue the books, had removed it, realising its rarity.

I could hear the faint jingling as Miss Wright came up the stairs again, as well as the clack of china on a tray. I slid the last volume back on to the shelves and stood up.

"Ha," the old man was gleeful, "that's very civil o' ye, ma'am. Returnin' good for our nuisance. I wonder if ye'd mind if we locked up this room an' had the police come along an' take a look at it."

It looked as though she was about to protest, but the Professor held up his square hand and went on.

"Ye'll understand, ma'am, that we don't want to trouble ye more than is necessary, but the sooner all these petty-foggin' details are dealt wi' the sooner ye'll find the police'll leave ye in peace." He changed the subject suddenly, "If it's not interferin' o' me, would ye mind tellin' me who inherits such property as yer uncle left?"

Miss Wright looked at him brightly. She did not seem to mind his interference. She passed him the sugar bowl.

"Oh," she said, and she looked pleased, "I expect that anything that Uncle Allan left will come to me. I'm his only living relative, and he's always promised that he would see that I was well provided for. You see, he was such a reasonable man and so very fair, that I still can't believe that this terrible thing has happened to him, and that the police have found out all these awful things."

Chapter 9

Suspect in Suspense

MR. CHARLES HUME arrived at the Chief Inspector's office with an escort. A small grey, predatory man accompanied him.

"Mr. Cowan, my lawyer," was all Hume said by way of introduction, and the Chief Inspector nodded briefly, his gesture giving the impression that he did not care whether Mr. Cowan was a solicitor or a dentist.

"Thank you, Mr. Hume," the Bishop said, without irony in his voice, "it is very kind of you to come along like this to help us."

Hume said nothing. His looks said nothing and the little blue eyes floating in their blood-shot puddles were not informative either.

The Professor sat on the chair which the Chief Inspector usually offered him. I think it must have been a relic of the days when Chief Inspectors were more generously built than they are today and that the Bishop must have dug it out of an attic in the Yard. It measured about three feet across the seat and had legs as thick as my biceps. So far as I could see the old man was not interested in anything that Mr. Charles Hume could say. He was reading Fitter's *London's Natural History*. I wondered why the hell we had bothered to come along. I guessed it was just that Professor Stubbs had an indefatigable curiosity which would not allow him to miss anything connected with a murder case in which he was interested.

"Now," the Chief Inspector was as suave as buttered asparagus, "Mr. Hume, I hope you feel rather more, let us say, communicative than you were yesterday afternoon. I would like to have fuller details of your business connection with Mr. Leslie than you have yet seen fit to give me. What exactly were these connections?"

He sat there giving a very good imitation of an expectant man.

Charles Hume said nothing. His bald eyes roamed round the room in a thoughtless way, much as the jaws of a gum-chewer work.

57

"Mr. Hume, my client," Mr. Cowan was precise, "feels under no obligation to answer any questions which you may put to him. He feels, and I may say is correct, that his business is his own affair so long as the police have no reason to suspect that it is run illegally. However, as my client is a reasonable man, he does not wish to put anything in the way of the police in the execution of their duties. My client is a very public-spirited gentleman. His connection with the late Mr. Leslie was merely that of one bookseller with another. While many booksellers advertise in their trade paper, called, I believe," he referred to a scrap of paper which, so far as I could see, was blank, "*The Clique*, it is natural that certain booksellers should, through the exigencies of their trade, come closer together and become more closely related than through the medium of a mere trade-paper. So it was with the late Mr. Leslie and my client. They had, over a period of years, learned one another's tastes and, in consequence, when one or other of them thought that he had something which might appeal to the other, he, naturally enough, informed the other about it directly, instead of choosing the quite unnecessary roundabout way of advertising in *The Clique*. If Mr. Leslie, for instance, wanted a book, he would perhaps ring up Mr. Hume to see if he had it, and the case was also *vice versa*. That is, in short, the measure of my client's connection with the late Mr. Leslie."

I had rarely heard a man say less at greater length. Mr. Hume's pale watery eyes were still exploring the beading on the ceiling. He did not appear to be interested in his lawyer's circumlocutions.

The Professor looked up from his book; he dug his hand in his pocket and found an envelope which he inserted to keep the place. He slammed the book shut.

"Harrumph, Mr. Hume," he snorted, "ye're about as helpful as a pond o' stagnant water. What d'ye know about a copy o' Evelyn's *Sculptura*, gi'en by him to Robert Hooke and since stolen, eh?"

Mr. Hume looked dispassionately at the old man. His little eyes rolled easily over the Professor's honest bulk. He shook his shoulders and his paunch sagged uneasily beneath the loose black suit.

"Nothing" he said unhelpfully.

The Chief Inspector was fiddling with a silver propelling pencil, twisting the lead slowly in and out. He snapped the lead between his fingers and looked directly at Hume. His voice was no longer weary. It held a suggestion of not very carefully hidden irritation.

"That is all very well, Mr. Hume," he snapped, "but we know that book to have been stolen, and when Professor Stubbs found it this morning among Leslie's possessions he also found a note connecting it with you. Can you explain this."

"No," Mr. Charles Hume was bored. His blue pig eyes were again wandering, inspecting the plasterwork of the cornice.

"Chief Inspector," Mr. Cowan was as sharp as a shrew, "I must ask you to explain further. What was this note connecting a stolen book with my client? Did it suggest that Mr. Leslie had obtained the book from my client?"

It was the Chief Inspector's turn to be silent. He carefully inserted a new lead into his silver pencil and slid it into position.

"That, I am afraid, is a question that I cannot answer at the present moment. I would just like to know what connection Mr. Hume had with the stolen book. Can you tell me that?"

"Sir," the lawyer was acid, "I may remind you that there is a law against slander in this country, and that, if you are suggesting that my client had anything to do with a stolen book you are on the verge of breaking that law. In fact, sir, I am not sure that you have not already passed from the strict line of what is permissible. It's intolerable, sir, that a man of the standing of my client, Mr. Charles Hume, who has had the misfortune to know a man who was murdered should be treated by you in this manner. I have a very good mind to call the matter to the attention of your superiors."

"All right," the Bishop was weary, "you can do that if you think it will do your client any good. I may say that, on the whole, an appeal to those above me is unlikely to produce much satisfaction. I am in charge of this case, and I have been in charge of other cases, and my superiors, as you call them, have never had any cause to complain of my conduct in working on a case. If it is of any amusement to you, however, you can report away, as much as you like."

"Gently son," the old man rumbled, "softlee, softlee catchee monkey. You won't make Mr. Hume dance by tread-in' on his corns. I'm thinkin' that Mr. Hume has somethin' he don't want us to discover. Well an' good. If he has, he's goin' the right way about makin' us try to find out all about it. I wonder what he's up to, eh, Reggie?"

This new gambit of the old man's, playing that Hume was not in the room was no more successful than the Chief Inspector's more direct approach had been. Mr. Charles Hume was about as voiceless as the giraffe. His vocal chords seemed to have atrophied and he seemed to be afraid of stretching them in case they broke. If silence was golden Charles Hume was a millionaire.

The predatory little lawyer picked up his hat, a stiff brimmed black homburg. He rose to his feet, dusting a speck of imaginary dust from the edge of his jacket. He turned to his client.

"Well, Mr. Hume," he observed brightly, "I'm afraid we're just wasting these gentlemen's time and I'm certain they are wasting ours. Good morning to you, Chief Inspector, and to you, sir."

He wagged his head at the Professor who wagged his in return. Mr. Cowan paid no attention to me; I might have been one of the office fixtures for all he knew.

For a moment I thought the Chief Inspector was about to make a move to detain them, but he apparently thought better of it. He went on twiddling the lead in and out of his pencil.

There was an appreciative silence in the room once Hume and his lawyer had gone. For all the impression they had left they might have been ghosts.

Suddenly the Chief Inspector grinned cheerfully. He looked like a man who was enjoying a private joke.

"What the hell's up wi' you, Reggie?" the Professor enquired in a peevish voice, "I didn't think ye got very far wi' that interview. In fact, if I may so wi' out bein' offensive, I thought Hume an' his dam' lawyer put it across you all along the line, eh?"

"Well," the Chief Inspector was thoughtful, "so far as events in this office were concerned they are no doubt thinking the same, but I've put a small bomb under Mr. H.'s feet. I wonder how he'll like it when he finds that I have obtained a search warrant, and that even now it's being put into effect. I had no difficulty in getting it, particularly after I announced your discovery of the stolen book tied up with his name. That wasn't really necessary though, as, on the whole, those up above me are pretty co-operative, and when I ask for something they know they're not running much risk in giving it to me. They damn well know that I wouldn't ask unless I'd a pretty good reason for it. After all, I'm a policeman and if I make a false step it can break me and I'm no more anxious for that to happen than any man is to lose his job."

The Professor chortled to himself as he filled his filthy little pipe and sent vile fumes swirling round the room.

"All the same," he said seriously, "I think you'll find that Mr. Hume is no fool. He don't impress me that way. I hope the men ye ha' on the job will be more careful than those on the search in Leslie's house were. If I was in Hume's position now, I'd not keep incriminatin' thin's lyin' around where any interferin' copper could stumble on 'em. Let's see now—where 'ud ye keep 'em, Max, if ye were in his position?"

"In a safe deposit," I replied promptly. I had been trying to think exactly what I would do if I was in Hume's position. After all the books were not a very bulky proposition and could be hidden almost anywhere. Shoved in among other calf-bound books on a shelf they would be quite likely to pass the notice of a casual searcher, though not of the police looking for them. On the other hand, it would be a simple matter to slip them inside bindings ripped off other books. This meant that the police executing the search warrant would need to examine every book in Hume's shop. I couldn't envy them their job. I said as much.

"Uhhuh," he grunted, "an' then the friend comes all over know that Hume has a safe-deposit, do we? Can ye check up on that, Reggie? Ye don't know if ye can, eh? Well, what the hell's the blinkin' blunderin' police-force for if it can't find a simple thin' like that, eh? Well, let's do a bit o' supposin'. Supposin' I'm Charles Hume," he looked vacantly at the cornice in a mad caricature of Hume's manner, "and I ain't got a safe-deposit, an' I don't like to lodge these thin's in the bank, where'd I hide them once I became kinda convinced they weren't handy objects to ha' lyin' about the house?"

"Perhaps," I ventured, "you'd leave them with a friend?"

"Uhhuh," he grunted, "an' then the friend comes all over moral when he hears that the coppers are lookin' for the books. No, no, Max, that's not good enough, not nearly good enough. Say ye wanted to hide them somewhere where ye could reach 'em almost any time o' the day ye wanted them, an' where no one 'ud ask any questions about yer wantin' them. Why, Max, it sticks out a mile. There's only one place where ye could hide them under these circumstances an' where ye'd know they were safe. Why, man, ye'd hide the dam' things in a suitcase at one o' the stations, in the left-luggage office. It's a cheap an' handy hidin' place, and pretty safe, too."

A pleased but tired smile was spreading Cheshire catwise across the Chief Inspector's face.

"Good, John, good," he said in a mildly patronising voice, "with a little practice you'll make a detective yet. I thought of that as soon as I had my warrant and I have men going round most of the stations at the moment trying to find a suitcase full of books."

The old man was indignant at this patronage. He blew out his cheeks like the frog in the fable.

"Dam' it all, Reggie son," he said mildly, "I find yer murderers for ye, an' I prove their guilt all for the love o' the game, an' ye sit back and grow fat on me exertions, an' ye have the thunderin' nerve to sit there like a dam' mandarin an' tell me I'll make a detective yet. Bah! Phooey! You go an' boil yer blinkin' head, an' serve it up as sheep's head broth. Bah!" I did my best to pour oil on troubled waters, but it seemed that the troubled waters were a fire and that I only made it blaze more fiercely. I finally managed to calm the old man down, however, while the Chief Inspector sat there smiling at him sleepily.

"Don't take on so, John," he said politely, "I know you're a marvel— a sort of combined Sherlock Holmes and Sexton Blake. But, you must admit that some of your solutions have come from your trying every possible solution till you hit on the right one. I seem to remember your telling me the story of Julian Huxley's monkeys, who were to be set down in front of typewriters, in the expectation that, by trying every possible combination of letters, they would eventually turn out the whole of Shakespeare's sonnets. Well, it sometimes seems to me that your detection works on the same principle."

"Son," the old man was pleased again, "you said somethin' there. Me, I got the scientific approach to things. I like to know what makes 'em work, an' so I take them to pieces, an' when I done that I look at all the pieces an' then try an' put them together again. I got a very mechanical mind. I don't miss anythin' because it don't seem to be o' importance at the moment. No, I look at everything carefully to try and see where it belongs."

"Sometimes," the Bishop was bland, "it seems to me that you put the pieces together wrongly, don't you?"

"Eh? Bah! It's not me fault if sometimes I can't understand how a thing goes an' so I do put it together wrongly. Then, son, I take it to bits again an' try another method o' approach. The things that ye think are due to luck, Reggie, are due to me havin' an incorrigably logical mind. I like things in their right places. I got a tidy mind."

The funny thing about this statement was that it is true. The old man may leave a holocaust behind him of jumbled papers and books, but when he comes to sit down to write a botanical paper, he has all the facts he wants carefully docketed and marshalled in his mind. It seems that the untidiness of his house is perhaps a compensation for the over exactness of his mind.

Even the Chief Inspector has to admit that for all his fluff and thunder, Professor Stubbs does manage to deliver the goods. He has no theories when he starts a case as to who might have done the murder. All the people concerned in it are equally under suspicion, or equally free from it. When he makes up his mind that someone was not the guilty party, he is usually right.

He parted from the Chief Inspector with great good feeling. He had justified himself. The Chief Inspector promised to ring him if anything occurred. The journey home was easy. The old man drove as if he was driving a load of spun glass. I have rarely known him so thoughtful about my feelings. The only trouble was that he did not seem to be thinking about me; he was building fancy theories in the air.

Chapter 10

Alibiless Lady

THE PROFESSOR'S dinner party was a success. How Mrs. Farley manages to produce such good meals beats me, but she does. We had eaten very happily and were sitting in the large work-room-library, sipping the old man's brandy and drinking coffee.

Gray leaned forward suddenly.

"I don't know how I can thank you enough, sir," he said, "that money you lent me yesterday will enable me to complete my purchase of these drawings, and I hope I'll be able to let you have it back in a week or two."

Mary Gray started to unwrap a small flat parcel which she had been clutching all evening.

"I thought, Professor Stubbs," she said gently, "that you might like this. We didn't like to come altogether empty-handed, after all your kindness to us."

"This," when she handed it to the Professor turned out to be a most charming water-colour drawing by Thomas Stothard, an illustration of the story of Ali Baba and the Forty Thieves. The old man beamed. He was as pleased as Punch. If there is one thing that really pleases him it is when someone gives him a present. When I feel I've been over tough with him I go out and buy a book for him and that calms things between us. Anyhow, he should have been pleased with the drawing. It was probably not worth very much, but it was absolutely charming and perfect in its minor way. I wouldn't have minded having it myself. I thought that, if everything else in the house had a way of filtering up to my rooms I would try and make certain that the drawing was one of the things that stuck there.

"Um," the old man was thoughtful as he pulled at his cigar, "Um. Ye know, Gray, I didn't invite ye an' yer charmin' wife here just to get ye to thank me for a kindness which I couldn't help doin' ye, nor did I ask ye in the expectation o' gettin' a drawin' as a present."

He picked up the drawing and looked at it with appreciation.

"No, son, what I wanted from ye was a bit o' explanation. I wanted to know what ye know o' Mr. Cecil Baird. It's a funny thing that all through this case we bin chasin' people who knew Allan Leslie, an' we more or less bin passin' those who might ha' known Baird."

Gray was not disturbed. He crackled the cigar the Professor offered him and absently lit it.

"Yes, sir," he said slowly, "I knew Baird, and I had no reason to like him. He was not an amiable character. He was one of those people who hangs about and makes money. The only dealing I, personally, ever had with him was about a drawing. He came into my office one day and looked through my drawings. He picked up a very fine early drawing by Augustus John, worth about seventy pounds, and said he would take it. That was fine, as the drawing had been picked up by Ellis Read, whom you met the other day, and he had not wanted much for it. The trouble began when I sent in my bill. I got a politely worded note from Baird saying that he was under the impression that I had given it to him as a present. I wrote back that I had had no such intention, and that I would be pleased to have the drawing back, as I had another customer who would be interested in it, and he would pay cash. Baird, still as polite as ever, wrote back and more or less said that if he heard anything further from me, he would inform the police that I was a dealer in obscene drawings and prints. I recollected that he had certainly looked at some rather near-the-knuckle things I had, and it seemed to me that it would be cheaper and less trouble to let him keep the drawing. After all it had not cost me much, and, though my conscience was quite clear, it would not have been pleasant, or good for business, to have had the police come pawing about in my cabinets and portfolios. So I decided that I could just count the drawing as a bad debt and let it go at that. You see, though I might have disliked Baird, I had no real reason to murder him. You don't murder a man because he diddles you out of some money, do you?"

"Hardly, son, not if ye're in a normal frame o' mind, an' I don't think ye're in anythin' else. No, no, I wasn't suggestin' that ye'd gone out on the spree an' had bumped off both Leslie an' Baird. I just thought that ye were holdin' back on him the other afternoon an' I wanted to know why."

"You see, sir," Gray was ingenuous, "I could not pretend that I had not used Leslie as a channel for disposing of awkward drawings and prints. I thought it was best to come absolutely clean there. But when

I realised that Baird had been murdered at the same time as Leslie and that I had had a to-do with him, well, sir, I remembered that I had nothing like an alibi. I didn't want to get mixed up in the case and so I played Brer Rabbit and lay low and said nuffin. It seemed to me to be the best thing I could do. It was pure bad luck that I'd had any contact with Baird at all. The man had a most unsavoury reputation that way. After I'd been diddled I thought I would try and find out a bit more about him. It seems that one of his tricks was to find something about a bookseller or dealer which he did not wish to have known. Then he'd go round to the chap's place and choose something pretty expensive and indulge in that sort of polite and unexceptional blackmail. There was nothing anyone could do about it legally. He wasn't so grasping that he would break a man, and it was usually cheaper and less trouble to pay up and be pleasant. You see, it would be difficult to explain to the police that a blackmailer had wanted drawings or books instead of money. They would more or less laugh at you for it. He was as safe as houses, or as safe as houses used to be before the blitz, and no one wanted to have the police fussing about their place. Oh, it was a neat trick all right."

I was admiring Mary Gray. She certainly was a winner. As her husband spoke she nodded.

"Ye knew all about this, Mary Gray," the old man turned to her. "Didn't it occur to ye that it would ha' bin better for yer husband to ha' told the Chief Inspector this when we met ye yesterday, eh?"

"Certainly, Professor Stubbs," she said softly, "I told Henry it would be more sensible to tell the police everything he knew. You understand that when Henry found out that Leslie had been murdered, he told me about his afternoon and about the fact that he did not think he could provide himself with an alibi. We thought of trying to fix one up for him. I would have sworn that he was in the office all afternoon. But then it occurred to us that there was just a chance that someone might have remembered seeing him, and if we had fixed up a false alibi and it was destroyed things would look ever so much worse."

"That was very wise o' ye, ma'am," the old man nodded his head and the mop of grey hair fell over his forehead. He swept it back with the edge of his hand, the hand that held the cigar. The hair sizzled briskly as it touched the glowing point and a faint smell of singeing pervaded the atmosphere. Professor Stubbs did not appear to notice this.

"Naturally," Mrs. Gray went on, "I would have done anything I could to help Henry, but you see, there was another point against my trying to fake an alibi for him. You see, I had not stayed in the office all afternoon myself. I went up to Selfridges—to buy an aluminium frying-pan. If I had started supporting Henry in saying we had both been in the office all the afternoon, the man in Selfridges' hardware department might suddenly have remembered me. You see, I did not take the pan with me, but asked them to send it to my address. If it comes to that," the idea had suddenly dawned on her, "I have no alibi either. I could easily enough have walked through to Wesley Street and back here in the time I was out. Selfridges was fairly crowded and I had to wait a long time to be served. I could have done the murders myself. I didn't like Baird and I didn't like Allan Leslie. Mr. Leslie was useful to Henry, but that was all. I would have been glad to see Henry give up the connection."

The old man had slumped himself down in his chair. He frowned at the point of his cigar.

"Hell," he said crossly, "it seems as though no one in this dam' case had anythin' in the way o' an alibi, except that little chap, what's-his-name from Bristol. If things go on at this rate I'll have to start suspectin' him as the only one who obviously couldn't ha' done the murder an' who consequently did do it."

He glared at me as if I was to blame for this state of affairs. I glared back as if to say that I thought his attitude most unfair. He relaxed.

"Can I take it from ye, ma'am," he addressed Mary Gray brusquely but with courtesy, "that ye didn't spend the afternoon in murderin' Leslie an' Baird, eh?"

Mary Gray smiled at him politely and sweetly.

"You can take it that way, Professor," she said gently, "provided you don't start proving that Henry did the dirty deed."

"Here, I say, Mary," Henry Gray was agitated, "don't you start making bargains like that. I've told you I didn't do the murders and you believe me. I know I didn't do them, and that's good enough for me."

Mary Gray looked at him with a look that said as plainly as words that she needed to look after him. It also said that she was very fond of him. Mentally I'd been toying with the idea of playing King David and casting Henry for the role of Uriah; I saw that I would have no complacent Bathsheba, so I gave up the idea. Certainly she was a peach of a girl. The sort of girl that makes me feel warm inside.

Professor Stubbs had finished his cigar and was engaged in scraping the black and tarry deposit from the inside of his little pipe. This is an operation that requires the utmost delicacy, as the pipe is so old that the least rough or careless handling of the knife might fracture its fragile charred walls. When he had completed the surgical operation to his satisfaction the old man took out a piece of plug and shredded it into the palm of his left-hand. He rolled the fragments of tobacco between his palms and tilted them into the bowl, scraping the reluctant fragments that stuck between his fingers out with the back of his pen-knife. He tamped the tobacco down with his thumb and placed the pipe between his lips. He lit his immense and rather frightening petrol-lighter. When the pipe was going to his satisfaction he leaned back and looked out through the clouds of smoke.

"O' course, ma'am," he said slowly, "Ye ha' now pulled yerself into the line o' suspects, but, for the moment, I'm not thinkin' that either ye or yer husband murdered Leslie an' Baird. I think I know who did the deed, but I'm not in a position to prove it yet. I don't know why it was done that way, nor do I know how the murderer went to work. Ye see, we got as far as knowing that the dead men were knocked on the head wi' a blunt instrument, but, when ye come to think o' it there's somethin' very odd about the case. Ye just don' walk into the back o' a shop an' knock a man on the head when there's another man there. Or if ye get away wi' that ye can't just turn to the other feller an' say, 'It's yer turn ole man—let me hit ye on the back o' the head.' Can ye see that actin' as a successful gambit for bumpin' off the second man. I can't. Yet, the doctor swears that they were both walloped on the back o' the nut wi' a blunt instrument. How d'ye think it was done?"

This question was addressed to me. I was always being given the hard nuts to crack. I didn't like it at all. I hadn't the foggiest idea how the murder had been done and I said so.

Here were two men, both of them knocked out by a blow on the back of the skull, lying in a room which was locked, or at least bolted, on the outside, while they puffed away at the gas which a kindly person had fed with a couple of bob. It was screwy.

"Umhum," the old man was going on, "well, let's say that ye are in league wi' Leslie to knock out an' rob Baird or the other way round. Well, ye knock out one and then wait till the other has started the job o' searchin' through his pockets an' ye take a wipe at him too. That seems to me to ha' bin the only way it could ha' happened, but ye see that we are still left wi' the problem o' why both were murdered. The only person we ha' yet found wi' a connection wi' both the deceased is Mr. Gray here, an', as he says, I don't think he's got a motive that would ha' made him do a murder. Also," he bowed to Mary Gray, "I may say that you got too much intelligence, ma'am, to allow yer husband to go out on a murderin' expedition, an' if things seemed so bad that a little bit o' murderin' seemed the only way out, well, I'd be willin' to bet, we'd find that ye'd rigged up a thunderin' good alibi for yer husband—not one that was so blinkin' watertight that an old man like meself would start nosin' around it, but one that was so nicely natural that no one would suspect it. If yer husband did this murder it's too blinkin' easy, an' I don't believe this is an easy case. I wouldn't be interested in it if it was. I don't like easy cases. I'm a reader o' thrillers an' I like those that I can't guess till I'm more than half way through."

His voice became rather querulous as he proceeded. He seemed to be about to continue his tirade, but the telephone jangled briskly. He leaned over to the little table on which it stood and disentangled its flex from the mass of books which had accumulated upon it. He took off the receiver and looked at the instrument as if half afraid that it might jump at him and bite. In spite of his love for all sorts of mechanical toys, I think the old man still has a sort of superstitious dread of the phone; he can never believe that it's real.

He steeled himself for the ordeal and bellowed at the mouthpiece.

"Stubbs here! . . . eh? . . . can't ye speak a bit clearer . . . damn it, man. I'm just whisperin' . . . eh? . . . what d'ye say? . . can't you talk a bit louder . . . don't treat the blinkin' phone as if ye were afraid o' it . . . grapple wi' it, man, like I do . . . eh? . . . it's you, Reggie, is it? . . . why the hell didn't ye say so at first instead of wanderin 'around tryin' to confuse me? . . . Ye got a titbit for me, eh? What do I make o' it? . . . Um, yes . . . well, I'm flummoxed . . . I dunno what to make o't . . . What do you? eh? Dammit, man, that's your business. Ye're a thunderin' copper. Ye just thought ye'd tell me to gi' me brain somethin' to work on while I slept. . . . All right, I'll be seein' ye in the mornin'."

He laid down the telephone with the triumphant air of the young Hercules discarding the strangled serpents. He looked at us with an expression which said plainly that he was the master of the phone and not its servant. I waited expectantly and, so I noticed, did Henry and Mary Gray. By virtue of long experience, I had learned that it was no good trying a direct approach. The old man loves to be mysterious. The only way to get round it was to play that it was of no interest to me.

"You were talking about detective stories," I said helpfully.

"Dam' it, Max," he exploded, glaring at me, "ye've no decent honest curiosity, ha' ye? That was the Chief Inspector. He thought it might interest me to know that Mr. Alister Macpherson—Hunter's alibi—shot himself at his home in Hampstead about a couple of hours ago. What d'ye make o' that, eh?"

Chapter 11

Grand Slam

AS WE entered the Chief Inspector's office in the Yard we met Miss Wright coming out. She was dressed in black material which rustled briskly as she walked, her feather boa was in place round her neck, she carried a short umbrella with a ridiculously large and shiny handle. I could have sworn that several more birds of the air and fruits of the field had come to rest on her hat since I had last seen her in it, but perhaps I was imagining things. That hat fascinated me; it seemed to be a sort of universal repository of all that was gaudy in nature. I suppose Miss Wright wore it as a compensation for the ungaudiness of her own face and figure.

She nodded to us politely and we went into the Chief Inspector.

"What'd she want?" growled the old man gesturing after her with his thumb.

"Oh," the Chief Inspector was amused, "she thought she should come and see me, as she wanted to know if it was all right for her to assume her uncle's death and proceed to try and tidy up his estate. I told her that so far as I knew her uncle was dead and that, as his heir, she had every right to proceed as she thought fit. She was almost over-whelmingly grateful. She didn't want to do anything which the police might disapprove of, and, as I was in charge of the case, she thought I should be consulted before she made any move. She confided in me that her uncle had carried a considerable amount of life assurances and she wanted to know whether the police were quite certain that her blessed uncle had not committed suicide. Not, of course, that she dreamed he had, but then I knew what insurance companies were, didn't I? I managed to assure her gravely that I was quite satisfied that her uncle had not committed suicide, and told her that the insurance people could apply to me. Funny old bird, isn't she? So sure of herself in one way, and yet so very uncertain in others. Terrified of getting into trouble with the police and very ashamed of her uncle's end. It seems that she is deeply concerned with what the neighbours would say. I tried to pacify her by pointing out that, after all, it was not her fault that Leslie was murdered and that none of the neighbours could blame her for it. 'Oh, no, Inspector,' she said, 'I quite understand that, but you know what people are. An unpleasant thing like this remains a slur upon the family.' I did my best with her and she seemed fairly satisfied."

The Chief Inspector laughed at the memory of the birdlike maiden lady fluttering in his office. Then his face became suddenly very tired again as he looked at the sheets of paper spread on the desk before him.

"As I told you on the phone last night, John," he began, "Mr. Alister Macpherson, at whose house the bookseller was working on the afternoon of the murders shot himself. He left a note which said that, with the death of Cecil Baird he could no longer continue. It took me quite a time to find out what this meant, beyond the obvious fact that he was one of Baird's victims. You see we have not yet found all Baird's papers, though a search for them is going on, and we found nothing which mentioned Macpherson beyond a small pocket-book which contains a list of names with ticks against them. The name Macpherson appears there, duly ticked, but without any indication as to which of the thousands of that name was meant. Of course, it is now obvious that Alister Macpherson was the man, but until this happened we had no line to go on. It was only when I was looking through Macpherson's papers that I stumbled on what Baird was blackmailing him about. He was an undischarged bankrupt, and if that had become known it would have meant immediate ruin. One of our chaps—an authority on City affairs—says that the company which Macpherson was running was as rickety as a bamboo chair. That would explain his anxiety to sell his library quietly. He wanted to raise money quickly, and he did not want it to get around that he was trying to raise it. I understand that his library is a very valuable one—at any rate there are the devil of a lot of books there."

"Um," the Professor looked unhappy, "well there's one point ye can get from that an' that is that it's thunderin' well certain that the late Mr. Macpherson had nothin' to do wi' the untimely decease o' Mr. Baird. However much Baird was stingin' him, he was more valuable alive than dead, eh?"

"Yes," the Chief Inspector brushed this obvious fact aside, "the trouble that now arises is whether Hunter's alibi still stands. The man who vouched for it is dead, and for all we know to the contrary Hunter may have known more about him than was obvious on the surface, and may also have been a victim of Baird's blackmailing activities."

"Uhhuh, that's more than likely," the Professor briefly outlined the story we had heard from Gray the previous evening.

The Chief Inspector folded his carefully manicured hands on the desk before him and inspected them moodily.

"There we go again," he said bitterly, "nice ordinary people getting mixed up in a murder and trying to dissociate it from themselves. They tell us half of the truth and will answer our questions truthfully enough, but they won't go out of their way to volunteer any information in case by so doing they become involved. Either that, or they fail to tell us the whole truth because it puts them in a bad light. I've nothing against Gray and his wife. So far as I'm concerned it's their own affair if they want to deal in dirty pictures. And I asked one of our people who is an authority on the suppression of obscene publications and so on, and he tells me that if the drawings were done by well-known artists there isn't a chance in hell of a successful prosecution. He told me some story about an exhibition of paintings by D. H. Lawrence which the police seized. He says they were perfectly within their rights in seizing them, but all the same the chap in charge of the seizure damned nearly spoilt his case by also seizing some reproductions of paintings by Blake which were lying around the gallery. He said that only two or three of the Lawrence paintings could be called really objectionable, but the others were nudes and the Blakes were nudes and so they were seized. It seems to me that a nude by a living painter can be called obscene, but a much more lascivious nude by a painter who is dead is a work of art. Seems to me there's something wrong somewhere."

"Uhhuh, there certainly is," the old man was forthright, "when a common copper can be set up as a judge of what is or what is not obscene. Bah! But this ain't gettin' us any further wi' the job o' solvin' the question o' who done it. I must say meself that I don't see Hunter crawlin' down from Hampstead, bumpin' off two men an' then crawlin' up again to get on wi' his valuation, d'ye?"

The Chief Inspector shook his head sadly.

"No, I can't say that I do, and, anyhow, Hunter has two witnesses as to his arrival at Wildwood Grove. The house table maid let him in, and the cook was passing the end of the hall at the time. And then the maid let him out again, after he had finished. I suppose we had better clear him out of the list of suspects for the moment. That leaves us with the two Grays, Ellis Read and Charles Hume. Now I don't like the man Hume. He's hiding something, but, till we can discover what that something is, we can't say whether he did the murders. My chaps haven't yet managed to bring anything to light. Hume was not what you would call co-operative when they made their search, but he did nothing which might be interpreted as impeding them. One of the fellows said he stood by, looking for all the world like a neutral country, on the side of the enemy, but not unwilling to tag along with you, just in case you won. The fellows who are trying the left luggage offices are not through yet, but I don't think Hume dare make a move. I've got a man watching him, and unless Charles Hume is a bigger fool than I'd credit him with being, he knows damn well that he's being watched, and so we can't expect him to make a false step and give himself away."

It was then I had my bright idea.

"Look here," I said suddenly, "I belong to a club called the Arts Theatre Club. You know it? Yes? Well I've often left bits of luggage in the cloakroom there, and have forgotten to collect it for weeks. Why I once left a pair of shoes in the place for more than three months. I was wondering where the hell I'd left them when the cloakroom attendant reminded me. What if Hume belonged to a club like that? He might just leave things there, as openly as he liked, and no one would think any more about it."

The old man beamed at me benevolently.

"Ye're coming along nicely, Max," he said in a kindly growl, "Ye'll be running down murderers before ye're finished."

I scowled at him. The trouble was that I did rather fancy myself as a detective, even if it did interfere with my ideal of the perfect quiet life. However, my wounded vanity was healed by the Chief Inspector.

"That's a first-rate idea, Max," he was really encouraging, "I'll put a man on to the job of following it up straight away."

He picked up one of the phones on the desk beside him and gave a short series of orders into it.

For the next hour the old man and the Chief Inspector chewed over the case from every possible angle. They all but persuaded me that I must have done the murders myself, for some motive which I had forgotten. They proved that every single person who was connected with the case was guilty and then, just as methodically, broke down the carefully erected barrier of guilt.

This was what the old man called his scientific approach. He enjoyed taking things to pieces. On the whole I think he is rather better at taking them to pieces than at putting them together again.

He and the Chief Inspector seemed to be enjoying themselves. They seemed to be playing a parlour game. In spite of the mild protests of the Chief Inspector, the Professor had started to prove that Miss Wright was the murderer. He was interrupted before he got very far with his fantasy. There was a knock at the door.

"Come in," the Chief Inspector looked up from the notes spread before him on the desk. "Oh, it's you, Jenkins. Well, any luck?"

It was a young plain-clothes man, with a small neat moustache. He looked very pleased with himself. He was carrying a large pig-skin brief-case which he held out to the Chief Inspector.

The case was locked. It looked a good lock to me, but it yielded to the gentle persuasions of a sergeant with a bit of bent wire. That man could have opened the Bank of England with a sardine-key.

The Chief Inspector opened the flap gingerly. I'm not ashamed to say that I leaned over him and peered at it. It was all right. The case contained several books. The Bishop took them out as carefully as if they were birds eggs.

The Donne *Anatomy of the World* was there and so was his *Pseudo-Martyr*. There was the copy of *Thel* by Blake. I looked at it carefully. I had never held a genuine Blake illuminated book in my hands before. It was certainly very beautiful. I could almost, for a moment, understand the temptation that would fall on a collector if the book was offered to him. It was such a beautiful piece of work that to have it in the house would be a continual pleasure.

But the list of treasures did not stop there. There was a copy of Herman Melville's *Moby-Dick*, in the original cloth and as fresh as the day it came from the binders. There was an *Alice in Wonderland* in the same condition, with an inscription by Lewis Carroll. There were several other treasures. Finally there was a pencil drawing. The drawing of a man with an odd face, receding brows and chin, before some fragments of stone or brickwork. The Chief Inspector just glanced at this. I seemed to be rather distinguishing myself that morning.

"Good Lord," I said, "do you know what that is?" The Chief Inspector shook his head. "That's Blake's drawing of *The Man who built the Pyramids.* It was stolen at an exhibition at Norwich to which it had been lent. It belongs to the Tate Gallery."

The Chief Inspector whistled softly to himself. That something was actually the property of the National Collection seemed to hit him a personal blow.

"Ha," he looked weary but the look was belied by his voice, "it looks as though Mr. Charles Hume would have quite a lot to answer for. Just imagine the man's nerve. Whew! Dealing in pictures stolen from the Tate Gallery."

He was examining the case very carefully. There was no doubt that it was the property of Mr. Charles Hume. It not only had his initials embossed in gold on the front of it, but it also contained papers and letters addressed to him.

"That's all right, sir," Jenkins spoke briskly, "the cloakroom attendant at the Burlingham Club, where I found this, is willing to swear that it is the property of Mr. Hume. He knows him well, sir, and says that he was frequently in the habit of leaving his case there for a day or two. Mr. Hume one day remarked to him that it was so much more convenient than leaving it in a station, as he could get or leave it there up till eleven o'clock at night."

The Professor was examining the recovered books with great interest. They were all in beautiful condition.

"Hmm," he said, "I'd like to know who the thief was. Whoever he was knew exactly what he was up to. None of your trimmed and dirty copies for him. No, he chose only the best. I wonder how the hell he managed to get away with it."

"That's one of the odd things," the Chief Inspector replied, "You'd have thought that the owners of the books would have been able to give some description of the thief, but not them. The trouble seems to have been that, say, one man would go in and look at the book, if it was in a bookshop. Then the chap would get talking to the attendant and someone else would pick up the book and walk off with it. We thought for some time that we might get a line from the people who asked to see the books. But that was an absolute flop. They all turned out to be well-known collectors, who were not only valued customers but in many cases personal friends of the booksellers. Several times it was the customer who noticed the loss before the bookseller. He turned round to pick up the book, saying either that he would have it or that it was beyond his purse, and discovered it was gone. We finally were forced to the conclusion that whoever was behind the thefts was a student of men, and knew something of the habits of these big collectors. He knew that many of them were in the habit of looking at a book and then laying it down while they thought the matter of its purchase over and spoke to the bookseller. He knew that they were unlikely to ask to see any book that was not worth having. Once he had worked out the scheme, the actual thefts could have been carried out by any expert pickpocket, part of whose business is to be so unobtrusive that no one notices him."

Chapter 12

Stalling Suspect

MR. CHARLES HUME was brought in by a policeman. His bald eyes flickered to the books lying beside his brief-case on the Chief Inspector's desk. They betrayed neither anxiety nor curiosity. His paunch swung gently as he seated himself upon the chair which the Bishop indicated.

"Mr. Hume," the Chief Inspector's voice was strictly official, "you have been taken into custody on a charge of receiving stolen goods. Do you understand?"

"Yes," said Charles Hume. It did not seem that he had shed his clam-like affinities.

"You also understand that you need say nothing unless you want to. I wondered whether you would care to make a statement."

"Yes," said Charles Hume, unexpectedly. I think the Chief Inspector nearly fell off his chair with surprise.

A police stenographer was quickly ready. We waited expectantly for Hume's statement. At least I did, and so, so far as I could judge, did the Chief Inspector. The Professor merely sat there chewing at his pipe and emitting clouds of poison smoke. He was still reading Donne's *Anatomy of the World*.

"These books," Hume indicated them with a thrust of his flabby arm, "belong to Mr. Leslie. Or at least they used to belong to him. He asked me to take care of them for him. He said they were valuable and that he was frightened of thieves. I was taking care of them for him. That's all."

As statements go, this one just about took the biscuit for the most unsatisfactory story on record. Even Charles Hume did not seem to expect us to swallow it. He sat there looking expressionless while the little blue balls of his eyes swam restlessly in their blood-shot ponds.

"Hey, son," the Professor leaned forward, "ye don't expect to get away wi' that, do ye?"

The blue marbles flicked towards the Professor who did not seem to be impressed either by them, or by the lack of hair around them.

"Look'ee here, son," he slammed one of his fists into the palm of the other hand, "a chap just don't gi' ye valuable books to look after for him, and then ye just don't go an' leave them in yer club, in an ordinary brief-case. It just ain't logic."

"Why should I not leave them in my club?" Hume enquired. "They were safe there. I've often left things there."

"Hell dammit, man," the old man growled, "ye know they were stolen. Ye're a bookseller an' every bookseller knew that these books were bein' sought for. Dam' it man, there's an advertisement for them in your trade-paper. Yet ye took the books, accordin' to yer story, from a man who's now dead an' who therefore can't gi'ee the lie. Ye took some books, knowin' they were stolen an' ye popped 'em into yer brief-case an' went away an' thought no more about it. Hell, son, go an' tell that to the horse-marines."

"I may have had some suspicions about the books," Hume was becoming positively garrulous, "but I had known Leslie for many years and had never had any cause to suspect his honesty. I took the books in good faith."

Looking across at the old man I could see that he was on the verge of exploding, volcanic, all over the Chief Inspector's office. I held up a finger warningly and he subsided.

"Yah!" his voice was quiet but insulting, "I bought the Koh-i-noor diamond from a stranger in the Strand. I did it all in good faith. Yah! Sir, I may say I don't believe yer story."

Charles Hume slid the blue balls towards him. His expression said that he did not care if the Professor believed him or not.

"I have made my statement," his voice was flabbily firm, like that of a man who could never make a decision suddenly making one. The Chief Inspector glowered at him sleepily across the desk.

"You know as well as I do, Hume," he said and his voice was quite disinterested and listless, "that no jury in the British Isles will believe your statement as it stands. Why don't you come clean and tell me what your connection with Leslie was?"

Mr. Charles Hume said nothing. He was an expert in saying nothing. If I had been handing out medals for being able to hold one's peace in difficult circumstances, Charles Hume would have had one with several bars. I looked at him with some interest. He looked a rather flabby, and not too clean man of about fifty odd. His face, as I have said was as hairless as a baby's bottom. I realised, with a feeling that there was something uncanny about it, that his wrists and the backs of his hands were covered with a thick black down. His suit did not fit him well; the jacket hung rather as though it was the overcoat of a rather smaller man and the knees of his trousers did not seem to have been acquainted with a presser's iron.

"I would be grateful," Mr. Hume's voice did not suggest that he could be grateful for anything, "if you would communicate with my lawyer and retail to him the questions you have asked me and the statement you have taken from me. You know his name. Here is his address."

He slid a card across to the Chief Inspector who ignored it for a moment while he made several notes on the piece of paper before him. Then he picked it up. His carefully manicured fingers held the piece of pasteboard with obvious distaste. They held it as though there was something insanitary and infectious about it. The half-closed eyes looked at it as though it could bear no message of any possible interest to Chief Inspector Reginald F. Bishop. I envied the Chief Inspector his command of this pose. I suffer myself from getting too excited over things and then I mess up the whole thing. The Chief Inspector held a straight flush in the shape of all the stolen books and the Blake drawing before him on the desk.

He laid down the card as if it was something which had nothing to do with the case in hand. He picked up the Blake drawing as carefully as if it had been made of finely blown glass. He looked at it with care for a moment.

"Odd looking drawing," he remarked uninterestedly, "you'd never think anyone would bother to steal it. Why I've seen as good drawings done by school children of fourteen."

I was just about to protest at this remark, but I saw that the old man was taking a leaf from my own book and was holding up a warning finger. I shut up. Someday perhaps I would be able to take the Bishop in hand and try and shew him what was a work of art and what wasn't. Till then I might as well hold my peace. I held my peace. It was difficult, but I managed it. The Chief Inspector was still looking at the drawing and at Charles Hume. He divided these activities in about equal proportions. Neither of them seemed to worry Hume. He sat there waiting for an answer to his request that the Chief Inspector should communicate with his lawyer. Nothing else seemed to interest him.

"Ho, yes," the Chief Inspector was thoughtful. He seemed to pay no attention to Charles Hume now, but merely looked at the drawing, "They say there's a fool born every minute. Well," he shrugged his shoulders with a gentle feline movement, "I suppose Mr. Hume knew where he would find a purchaser for this drawing. Hmm," he half closed his eyes and looked at the drawing sideways. I don't think that made it look any better to him, "and Boyle assures me that this drawing is the property of the Tate Galley. He swears he'd know it anywhere. Says it was left to the National Collection by Miss Alice Carthew in 1940. Well, of course, I'm a simple man and wouldn't know about such things, but I'd be willing to take his word for it. And further when I rang up the gallery, Mr. Robin Ironside seemed to be most excited and wanted to know how we'd found the drawing. I suppose Mr. Boyle and Mr. Ironside both know what they're talking about eh, Hume?"

He shot the last remark directly at Hume, like a pea blown by a boy expert. It bounced off Hume's skin like a pea would have done. He seemed to have been slightly stung by the shot, but quite unhurt.

"I wouldn't know," he replied loftily, his blue eyes wandering over the papers on the Chief Inspector's desk, "These things are above me. I'm a bookseller and don't know anything about drawings."

"No, son," the old man suddenly came to life again, "I'd say ye didn't—not unless there was some money to be made from them. I'll suggest to ye, to use the legal terminology, that the trouble wi' ye is that ye're hoping some blinkin' miracle will turn up which 'ull save ye from everythin'. Ye don't want to be concerned in the murders o' Baird and Leslie—ye don't want to admit that ye've bin handlin' stolen goods. Ye're playin' a dam' fool Micawber—waitin' for somethin' to turn up. Ye can take it from me, son, it won't, it never does when ye most need it."

Hume looked as though he was about to make some reply to this outburst when the telephone rang sharply in the room. The Chief Inspector picked it up carelessly. His expression did not alter as he intoned into the microphone in a sad and weary monotone. He rang off.

The Bishop looked at Hume blandly. Hume was obviously disinterested. I thought the pose was beginning to weigh on him. His look of complete dissociation was beginning to wear thin.

"That," the Chief Inspector spoke with the solemnity due to his position, "was a friend telling me to pick up someone of the name of

Bert Gorman, who, I believe, enjoys some local reputation as a pick-pocket. My informant assures me that he will tell me all about these book thieves and, also and especially, to whom they sold their loot. Have you any comment to make on this, Hume?"

The little blue fish swam back from the corners of the room. They settled locust-wise on the figure of Chief Inspector Bishop. They did not like to see him; in fact, the sight of the Chief Inspector seemed to worry them so much that they swam off round the room again.

"Me?" said Mr. Charles Hume in a surprised voice, "me? What should I know about a pickpocket? I'm a bookseller."

There was no immediate answer to this.

The Chief Inspector tried again.

"Hume," he said, "you know that the game's up. There's no point in your trying to hold out any longer." He picked up the telephone on his desk and spoke briefly into it, "I want to see a pickpocket of the name of Bert Gorman. What's that? You think you can pick him up within half an hour. All right. Bring him to me when you find him."

He turned round to Hume again. The blue eyes were watching him closely. The pink round them seemed to be slightly more suffused with red. Charles Hume moved uneasily in his chair and his paunch swayed with his movements. His large flabby hands still lay flat and unworried on his knees. They were as white as if they had been modelled out of baker's dough.

"I have nothing to add to my statement," he said, "only I would like to make it clear that there seems to be a plot in hand trying to involve me. I want to see my lawyer."

The Chief Inspector picked up the fragment of cardboard which lay discarded on his desk. His face shewed his distaste. He rang the number and spoke into it for a moment. Then he laid down the telephone.

"Mr.—er—" he consulted the card unnecessarily, "Cowan will be along within a few minutes, Hume. Should you have anything to say before he comes this is your chance. I may say that, personally, I do not think that you have a chance in a million of, as they say, beating the rap. Once you have consulted with your lawyer, all you will do is to tie yourself up more firmly than ever."

The Professor again leaned forward and examined Charles Hume with interest.

"I say, son," his voice boomed suddenly in the small office, "'Ud ye mind tellin' me what ye know o' Cecil Baird?"

The small blue eyes edged slowly down from the cornice, where they had apparently been admiring the plaster-work. They rolled round till they came to rest on the Professor's face.

"I have never heard of him," Hume said, and then corrected himself, "or at least I have never heard of him until I read that he had been found murdered along with Leslie."

"He wouldn't ha' bin blackmailin' ye, would he? He wouldn't ha' found out that ye were dealin' in stolen books an' ha' turned that information to his own use, eh?"

"No," said Charles Hume firmly, "I had not heard of him until the other day."

The Chief Inspector was thumbing his way through a little black morocco leather note-book. He found what he wanted and looked up at Hume. The eyes had again drifted into the corners of the room.

"That's odd, Hume," he said and his voice was surprisingly crisp, "he has your name down here with a tick against it. I wonder," his tone was reflective and sleepy again "why he did that. Where we have found these ticks elsewhere in the book we have found that the name tallies with one of his victims, from whom he had collected either money or goods. Can you explain that?"

"No," said Hume. His attitude was now one of collapse. His body seemed to be melting into the chair like a jelly placed on a hot plate. Still he refused to admit anything. The Chief Inspector gave it up.

We sat in silence waiting for the arrival of the lawyer. I noticed that Professor Stubbs was busily engaged in playing noughts and crosses against himself on the back of an envelope with a tiny butt-end of pencil. His habit of breaking all pencils into pieces about an inch and a half long annoyed me. I kept on buying pencils for the house and supplying the old man with new ones, nicely sharpened, but before he had used a pencil for ten minutes he would snap it across between his blunt fingers and would then proceed to trim the fragments neatly into new small pencils, too short for him to break.

The Chief Inspector made a few more notes on the paper before him. I sat and watched Hume. He sat there saying nothing and breathing a shade heavily. I realised that the blue stains round his mouth and nostrils indicated a bad heart. I wondered how he would stand up to any shock and didn't think he would take anything in the way of a surprise well. He was too loosely fat and flabby. In bulk he was nearly the equal of Professor Stubbs, but the Professor, for all that he claimed to be a tired old man, was as hard as the proverbial bag of nails.

The door of the Chief Inspector's office opened and a constable shewed in Mr. Cowan. He advanced into the room removing yellow gloves.

"Ah, Mr. Hume," he said, shewing a yellow tooth, "this is too bad. What's the trouble this time?"

Hume said nothing. The Chief Inspector explained the position in a few moments.

"I must consult with my client," Mr. Cowan was businesslike, "can you put a room at our disposal?"

The Chief Inspector nodded. He rang a bell and Mr: Cowan and Charles Hume left the room with a constable as escort. Hume shook like an aspen as he rose to his feet. His unfriendly little blue eyes flickered round the room, touching each face in turn. He said nothing.

As he went out he came face to face with someone in the corridor.

"Hullo, Chas," the voice said, "they've caught up with you at last?"

Chapter 13

Picking Brains

THE MAN who was shewn into the Chief Inspector's office was not noticeable in any way. He would have passed without mention in a crowd. His clothes were good, but not too good, smart enough but not flashy. His height was medium and his face was the face of one of the crowd. In fact he was a walking example of natural camouflage.

He might have passed either as a clerk at two hundred and fifty a year or a managing director at five thousand. It depended entirely upon the way he carried himself.

At the moment he was in a state of comparative relaxation. His face was wreathed in smiles.

"Hullo, Chief," he greeted the Bishop, "hope I ain't been doing anything which brings me into your department. I'm an honest pickpocket I am. So when the busy picks me up and says 'Come along, me lad, Chief Inspector Bishop wants to see you,' I says it's a fair cop and comes quietly. I don't want to get mixed up in no murder cases, not me. Ugh."

He shuddered elaborately. The Chief Inspector looked up at him.

"Well, Bert," he said listlessly, "I know you, and I know your habits. If you know what's good for you you'll come clean. What was your position with regard to Mr. Charles Hume?"

Gorman made a face of astonishment. It didn't seem to be real astonishment, but rather what he seemed to think was expected from him.

"Who split?" he asked and gestured towards the door. "Him? Chas? He'd a good racket and now it's gone sour on him. Who was the nose?"

"Never mind, Bert," the Chief Inspector was business-like, "I'm asking the questions—what did you do for Hume?"

Gorman shrugged his shoulders. He seemed to be thinking of stalling for time, but finally made up his mind.

"Mind if I sit?" he asked, taking a chair. "It's a fair cop and I'll come clean. Chas thought up a fine racket and I worked with him in it. My job was to follow a big bug—Chas would pick him for me—into a bookshop and hang around. If he asked specially to see any book which the bookseller had to get out of the safe or from some special case, I'd hang around and see if I could get me forks on it. After that, presto, the book was in Chas's hands. He paid me well for my work and he never grumbled if the book wasn't worth all that he'd hoped it would be. It was a fine racket," his voice was regretful as he realised that it had finished, "as none of the ordinary fences would touch the stuff and nobody suspected Chas. Oh, he's a smart one, Chas is. I wasn't the only one he had on the game, I know, as some of the stuff was burglar stuff and I don't touch it. All above board and the quickness of the hand deceives the eye is my motto."

The police stenographer was busily taking all this down. Gorman spoke very fast and with a considerable display of gesture, as if he found it a relief to be able to accentuate his words with his hands without appearing out of character.

"I suppose you know what this means?" the Chief Inspector asked.

"Me," Gorman was indignant, "of course I know. But it was a fair cop and I'll do my stretch. I done it before and," his smile was engagingly impertinent, "I don't doubt I'll do it again. All I want to do is to keep yours truly out of anything to do with a murder-case. I know that Chas was mixed up with Leslie and I don't want to let Mrs. Gorman's little boy get mixed any more than he has to. See?"

The Chief Inspector nodded. The Professor set back letting the thick smoke from his pipe drift round him. like an unearthly shroud. I just sat and twiddled my thumbs.

"I got an alibi for the time of the murder," Gorman went on, "I was with Chas."

I nearly fell off my seat. I had slowly been convincing myself that somehow the fat and slug-like Chas Hume had murdered Baird and Leslie. The Chief Inspector seemed to be surprised too. He snapped the lead in his silver propelling pencil. Only the old man sat there looking as if nothing could surprise him, and, in fact, rather as though he had expected something like this.

The look of pleased self-satisfaction on his face annoyed me. If he hadn't been my boss I'd have felt tempted to wipe it off for him. I began to regret once more that I had cancelled my holiday. Here I was sitting on a hard deal chair in a stuffy office, inhaling the poison gas fumes of the old man's pipe, when all the time I might have been lying in the sun in the Scilly Isles.

The Bishop readjusted the lead in his pencil and looked up at Gorman.

"Yes?" he said enquiringly.

"You see," Gorman was childlike in his pleasure, "I'd laid my fingers on a book in—" he named a large bookshop off Bond Street, "and I took it back to Chas. He looked it up in a book and told me I'd done well. He said it was so perishing rare that most collectors would give their pants to get it. He said there were only two other copies recorded. What was it called? Oh, it was a little book in dirty old leather. It's name was something to do with anatomy and it was by an old fellow called Don. I knocked off another book by him recently too."

He was very pleased as he recollected his prowess. The slighting reference to the Donne *An Anatomy of the World* was very amusing. Hume had certainly been very clever. His tool was a man who knew nothing about books, but then he didn't need to. The beautifully simple thing about the game was that it all depended upon the tastes, mostly expensive tastes, of men who were great collectors and who could be relied upon to look for books that were worth having. All Hume had done was to fix a tail on to their brains. In fact, he had made the great collectors his cat's paw to pull the chestnuts towards him. The audacity and simplicity was astonishing.

"Harrumph," the old man cleared his throat with a noise like the beginning of the Last Trump, "d'ye mean to tell me, Mr. Gorman, that ye just took anythin' any o' these people chose?"

"Yes," said Gorman, "it was easy. They'd pick on the book. Look at it for a bit, turn it this way and that in their minds, and then they'd lay it down, while they spoke to the bookseller about the weather or about an auction at Sotheby's or something of the kind. Neither of them would pay any attention to the book which was lying beside them. So I just used to walk past them and pick the book up as I went by. I sort of collect things like that by some kind of magnetism," his tone was apologetic but satisfied. "They never noticed me as I went past. You see, I've been a long time in the game and I've got so that people don't notice me. They may have an impression that someone has passed them, but ninety nine times out of the hundred they couldn't give you an idea what I look like. The tall ones have an impression that I'm a short man, and the dumps think I'm tall. Of course, there's always the chance that someone will catch you in the act, but then I'm careful. Careful Bert Gorman I am. They don't often catch me, do they?"

He appealed to the Chief Inspector who glanced at the sheet before him which contained Gorman's record.

"No," he said, "they don't often catch you, Bert. Four stretches in nearly twenty years isn't a lot."

"There, you see," Gorman smiled round at us, "you see I'm careful. If I think there's a chance of being nobbled, well I just let things slide. There's many as clever as me in the racket, but there's few who take as few risks. If I see a guy with a gold watch and think I'll put the finger on him, I look around and see that there's no chance of anyone else watching me do it. If there's anyone around who might be smart enough to tumble me, well I just don't bother about the ticker. I let it go and tell myself it was probably rolled gold and out of order, that the guy was only wearing it for swank."

"Uhhuh," the old man was drinking this in as if it had been a quart of beer. "So ye just did exactly as Hume told ye to do, eh?" Gorman nodded pleasantly. "An' he paid ye a standard sum for everythin' ye brought in, eh?"

"He always gave me fifty nickers for anything," Gorman replied, "but when I brought in anything extra good he'd give me a bonus. For that dirty little Don book he gave me an extra fifty. I liked working for him, for he never said that a book was no damned good to him and left it on my hands. No, the book might be a mistake and only worth a fiver, but he came across with the fifty all the same. What he lost on the roundabouts he said he made up on the swings."

He stopped and looked round at us. His attitude became rather defensive.

"You don't think I'm splitting on Chas, do you?" he asked pugnaciously, "I'm no copper's nark. I just don't want to be mixed up in a murder and it was a fair cop. Anyhow you got Chas first. What did he spill? You don't think I'm a mouth, do you, Chief?"

"No, no, Bert," the Chief Inspector was reassuring, "I don't think you're a nark. All that we've got from you we could have got from Hume, and once he was frightened he'd have dragged you in quick enough. Now, I would like you to give me some details of what you call your alibi for the time of the murder."

"Well," Gorman spoke more carefully, "I'd knocked off that Don book a couple of days before, but I hadn't been round to see Chas with it. I always used to let it lie for a couple of days before I took it to him. That was his order and I stuck to it. He was the brains, wasn't he? And, by god, he had the brains all right. Well I went round to him, carrying the book inside the binding of another book. If there was anyone in the shop I'd just hold it out to him and say, This is an old book which I found in the house, I wonder what it's worth. It's two hundred years old.' He would look at the book and say, 'I'll give you seven and six for it,' or maybe it was half a nicker. I'd say 'Oh I expected more than that. It's a very old book. I've got a lot more like it at home.' He'd say, 'A lot of old books aren't worth much, but if you've got any more I'd be pleased to see them.' Then he'd hand me the half nicker and I'd leave the shop. I'd go all the way back home and collect two or three more old books which he'd supplied me with. These were his orders. He said he was being careful in case he was watched and that was O.K. by me. I'm careful myself. If there was anyone still in the shop he'd ask me to leave the books and call back in about half an hour when he'd have time to look at them. I'd buzz off to a Lyons or a boozer, depending on the time of day, and fill in the time. Then I'd go back and he'd either be alone or he'd say 'I can give you a pound for these books, but this one's no use to me.' He'd hand me the quid and the book. Inside the book was the fifty nickers. There was someone in the shop that afternoon, but when I came back the second time Chas was alone. It was then he told me I'd done very well and gave me the extra fifty. Oh, it's no use your thinking, Chief, that you'll get it back. It all went down the drain on a pony yesterday. Marigold was her name and I thought she was a dead cert at seven to one and I plunged on her. Finish, napoo," he spread his hands in an expansive gesture. "Well, I hung around chatting with Chas for about half an hour and then I went out for a drink, for I'd promised to meet some of the boys in a club up West. Chas seemed a bit worried about something."

"Do you know what he was worried about?" the Chief Inspector asked.

"Well, he asked me what I knew about a man called Baird. 'Don't you touch him Chas,' I said, 'he's dirt. He stinks so bad a skunk leaves the room when he comes in.' Chas said he knew that, but did I know anything about him. I had to say I didn't. There were precious few who did not know anything about him. I knew he was in the black and would give a good price for letters and so on if they were of use to him, but, though I've found quite a lot of that in wallets I've knocked off, I won't touch the black. It's a dirty game."

Curiously enough, Gorman's face shewed no pride in his unwilling-ness to help a blackmailer or to profit by his knowledge of someone's indiscretions. He made the statement that Baird was dirty as he might have mentioned the fact that a horse on which he had betted had lost. It seemed to be natural to him to keep away from what he considered to be filth. Sneak thief though he might be I couldn't help feeling a certain respect for him. He would steal a man's wallet, but he'd sooner serve a stretch than profit from anything he found in it, except money.

"That's all right, Bert," the Chief Inspector said, "we know you are a clean thief. Did Hume say any more to you about Baird?"

"No," Gorman was thoughtful, "but I kind of got the idea that somehow Baird had tumbled to Chas and was trying to sweat him. That was like Baird. He'd take cash from anyone. He was just plain dirt. I'll bet there weren't many tears shed for him around town. I know a lot of fellers who'd have been glad to knock him on the head and who would then have danced on his grave. He'd sometimes take stuff off a chap, who'd lifted it, and then refuse to pay for it, saying it had been stolen. Myself I thought that those who dealt with him got what they deserved. But, you see, he only did this sometimes, and at other times he'd pay a good price, so, if you were dirty enough not to mind the black, you took the risk of offering it to him."

A constable knocked on the door.

"Excuse me, sir," he said, "Mr. Cowan has asked me to tell you that Mr. Hume is ready to make a statement."

"All right," the Chief Inspector said, "bring him in in a minute." He turned to Gorman, "All right. I'll see what I can do for you. It's not much I'm afraid but I'll do my best."

"Thank you, Chief," Gorman rose to his feet, "I'll do nicely. Go easy on old Chas if you can. He was good to work for."

Bert Gorman was removed by a constable. In a way I was sorry to see him go. He had been an amusing witness, with his own code of morals.

The door opened and Hume, escorted by yet another constable, came in, followed by Mr. Cowan.

"Chief Inspector," Cowan lifted the corner of his mouth to reveal a yellow tooth, "on consultation with my client, I have advised him to withdraw the statement which he made earlier this morning. He is now prepared to make another. I wish it to be understood that he does this of his own free-will. I strongly advised him against doing so, but Mr. Hume insists."

Charles Hume was quivering as if he had been hit by an icy draught. He lowered his quivering bulk and his swinging paunch on to a chair. His blue eyes were fixed in their red seas. He looked as though he had been weeping.

He started to speak slowly, and carefully. His statement bore out everything which we had been told by Gorman. It incriminated one or two other criminals, a burglar and a professional shoplifter. Gorman had guessed right when he said that he thought that Baird was blackmailing him.

When Hume had finished his statement the fact stood out that, no matter though he was guilty of organising the thefts, it was quite clear that he had had no hand in the murders. One or two facts would have to be checked but none of us had the least doubt of his innocence on that count.

Chapter 14

Down in the Junk

CHARLES HUME had gone. He signed his statement in a quavering hand, sent his blue eyes on their last quest round the office and was removed.

All this time the Professor had been sitting like a graven image. I could see that the unusual role of spectator was beginning to irk him. He hoisted himself out of the chair and yawned hugely, disclosing a cavern that seemed large enough to hold most of the office furniture. This cavern he tried ineffectually to cover with a short blunt finger.

"Hmm," he glowered at the rosy-pink and sleepy Bishop, "Who put ye on to Gorman, eh?"

The Chief Inspector smiled.

"I thought you'd ask that, John," he said, "I saw the question bursting out of you as I laid down the phone. No, you needn't guess. It was Mr. Ellis Read, talking from a public call office. He said he would be at his cellar in Marchmont Street if we wanted him."

"What are we waiting for?" the old man howled, "let's go visit him."

He swept us from the Chief Inspector's office and into the Bentley before we had time to think about it or to protest. The Bentley was roaring before I had really had time to get my breath. Once we started I did not dare to open my mouth as the blast of air would have held it open for the rest of the journey.

The old man parked the car at the entrance to Marchmont Street, in Bernard Street, and plodded straight across the road into a pub. By the time the Chief Inspector and I had climbed out of the car and had followed him at a more sedate pace, he was already sinking his second pint of bitter. Pints stood on the bar, creamy topped, waiting for us.

"Cor," he said coarsely, "anyone 'ud think ye weren't thirsty. I bin dying for a drink for hours, sittin' in that stuffy little office an' listenin' to everyone talkin' their heads off. Cripes, Max, how often I got to tell ye I dehydrate quicker than the ordinary man. I get dry. I need a drink an' all you fellers think of is goin' ahead in a parched condition. Beats me how ye do it. So far as I'm concerned this army marches on its thirst, from one pub to the next. I'm thinkin',," he leaned towards me with a conspiratoral and villainous air, "o' fittin' up a pint o' beer in the back o' yer car. That's the trouble wi' all this detectin'—it's dam' thirsty work an' no one but meself realises it."

The Chief Inspector drank his beer slowly. He is not by nature a beer-drinker, being a lover of the more refined pleasures of life. I drank my beer at a normal rate. I cannot pretend to keep up with the old man. If I tried I would die a sodden wreck before I reached my fortieth birthday.

I recalled the scandal the old man had once caused by turning up to give a lecture on plant physiology carrying a quart mug and six quart bottles of beer.

"Ladies an' gentlemen," he had explained with a bellow, "it's goin' to be thirsty work talkin' to ye, so I came prepared. I at least will not be dry though ye may grow so watchin' me. On the other hand, I couldn't bring enough beer wi' me to go round. All I can suggest is that we get through this dam' lecture as quick as possible an' that ye ask thunderin' few questions. If ye do that we may make the Blue Pig across the road before closin' time."

He laid the bottles out before him on the lecturer's table, and used his mug to beat on it as a signal to the man working the magic lantern that he wanted another slide. The lecture was an immense success and the old man had to drive the magic-lantern chap home, as he insisted it was his fault that the fellow drank so much after it. That was quite true. It was. He insisted that working a magic-lantern must be even thirstier work than talking.

The Chief Inspector laid down his empty mug with the air of a man who had kept right on to the end of the road. I had had three pints. I wouldn't like to guess what the old man had had.

We wandered up Marchmont Street. Near the top we found Ellis Read's cellar. We had to descend by a narrow stone staircase into the basement. The old man just managed to squeeze himself between the rickety iron banister and the wall as he lumbered down it. He beat heartily on the door facing us.

The door opened and Mr. Ellis Read faced us.

"'Ullo, 'ullo, 'ullo," he said, "regular family party, eh? Come in and make yourselves at home."

The whole of the basement was occupied by piles of books and heaps of canvasses. We squeezed our way through these into a small room at the back where there was a trestle-table. Before the table a seat had been made up from piles of volumes of the *Studio* and the *Burlington Magazine*. The top of the table was covered with pens and water-colour paints and brushes. A large book lay open among them. I recognised it as the copy of Thomas Shotter Boys's *London* which Read had said he was colouring.

"Take a seat, gentlemen," Read's gesture was expansive, but there were no seats in the room. "Come on, gents, make yourselves at home. Sit on a pile of papers, sit anywhere. You won't hurt the things, not you. This is only junk. I know. That's my business."

I perched myself, rather precariously, on the top of a mound of magazines, which tumbled this way and that every time I moved. The old man, with a regal air, advanced to the more or less secure heap before the table and planted himself there. The Chief Inspector was left balanced on the top of a pile of old and decrepit picture frames. Mr. Read left the room for a moment. He reappeared holding a shooting stick. Judging from the elaborate basket-work of the seat on this and its general unwieldiness it must have dated from the early nineties. He opened this carefully, drove the spike into the rotten boards of the floor, and seated himself.

He looked round us expectantly.

"Now what can I do for you gents," he enquired cheerfully, "I'll find you anything you want. That's my business."

"Mr. Read," the Chief Inspector's tone was not over cordial, "I would like a little more information from you. It seems to me that you know rather more about this case than you have so far admitted. How did you know that Bert Gorman was the book thief employed by Charles Hume?"

"Lord bless you, sir," Read was amused, "I know that kind of thing. You see," his voice became confidential, "that's my business. I know everyone in the trade and everyone knows me. Well, sir, bless you, I knew you'd been questioning Charles Hume. I know that kind of thing. It gets around. Then I remembered seeing Gorman there once or twice, and I also remembered seeing him hanging about Quaritch's. So, you see, sir, it was simple. I know the trade. That's my business. I know that Gorman is a pickpocket. How do I know that? Why, bless you sir, he's known as one all round the West End. So last night I says to myself, 'Ellis, my boy, there's been a lot of stealing going on recently, and you know that Mr. Hume is mixed up in it and you know that Gorman is a pickpocket.' Well, there you are, sir, I just put it all together and it came out right. It was just like supplying a good leaf for a book that has one missing. It was a matter of finding the right things and putting them together. That's my business."

"Uhhuh," the Professor grunted suddenly, "you're one of the fellers whose business it is to be in the know, eh?"

"Exactly, sir, exactly," Read turned to him, "you have got it quite right. If you live as I do from your ability to find things for people you soon learn whom you can trust and whom you can't. There are some firms, now to whom I always allow credit. That is I take in what I have found and leave it there even if I don't get paid for it immediately. I know they'll pay me whenever I want the cash. I use them, in fact, as a convenient bank. But there are other firms, and you'd be surprised if I told you their names, for whom I will do a job of work, but from whom I expect immediate payment. That's my business. You see, sir, I need to have my capital at call any time I want it, and if a firm wants to hold back to the end of the month it just doesn't suit me. Why, sir, bless you, only the other day I saw a Stubbs in a sale at Edmonton. I thought it might fetch a hundred and even there I thought I'd make a profit, so I collected a hundred by going round the firms I call my banks. I got the painting for twenty quid and it was dirt cheap at that. But I have to know where I stand. That's my business."

"Umph, Mr. Read," the old man growled in a friendly way, "I see. You want to know all about everyone connected with what you call 'the trade,' is that right?"

Read beamed at him. His facial expression said that the Professor was picking it up quickly.

"Umm," the Professor as was his habit suddenly switched the subject, "what d'ye know about a character o' the name o' Cecil Baird then?"

Mr. Read looked pained. His face took on a look of the most extreme disapproval.

"I would hardly say, sir, that he was connected with the trade. He was a scoundrel, sir, a dirty blackmailer. During the war, bless you, sir, there were a lot of low characters who crept into bookselling and publishing. It looked like a good racket to them. They have mostly drifted out of the trade again, sir, and good riddance to them says I. Baird was mixed up in one of those wartime publishing rackets. Their game, sir, was to publish cheap near pornography on black-market paper. They failed, sir. They didn't understand the traditions of the trade. I knew all about Baird, sir, bless you, as soon as I saw him. His racket was the tough imitation American gangster thriller in which girls have their

clothes torn off. Harmless enough stuff, I may say, sir, but I didn't like
Baird. Since then, sir, he has come out openly as a crook. He's a blackmailer, sir, or rather I should say he was a blackmailer. He would buy
secrets from discharged and disgruntled assistants and would turn them
to his own use. He knew too much, I always said someone would
knock him on the head one of these days. He deserved to die if ever a
man did. But, sir, however crooked Mr. Leslie was, sir, he was an honest man. He paid up on the spot, sir, and was forthright to deal with.
Mr. Hume now, sir, he was a good man too. He thought of a good
game and he used it. I can't approve of one member of the trade rob-
bing another member but all the same Mr. Hume was good to deal
with. Neither he nor Mr. Leslie haggled with me over prices. They
knew that I asked a fair price and made a fair profit. That's my
business."

The Chief Inspector seemed to be getting restive. I could hear the
wood of the frames grating beneath him as he moved on the pile. Small
flakes of gesso and gilt were falling on the floor. I sat as still as I could
as if I dared to shift cascades of old magazines slid to the floor.

"Now, Mr. Read," he said and his voice was authoritative. "I would
like you to tell me all you know about Mr. Leslie."

"Why bless you, sir, I didn't know much about him. He was the sort
of man who always kept himself to himself and wasn't what you might
call forthcoming. He bought books of all sorts from me, for he had a
lot of University gentlemen among his customers, but he never said
much about himself. I knew he was a good market for banned books
and for any drawings that were what you might call out of the ordinary.
It's my business to know these things. So when I found anything which
I thought would interest Mr. Leslie I just took it along with me. He
treated me fair sir, that he did. Gave me what I asked and never tried
to beat me down. Any of those in the trade who know me will tell you
that I ask a fair price for what I find, a price that'll leave them a fair
profit. They know who they are dealing with. And on my side, sir, I
like to know where I stand. That's my business. Mr. Leslie paid me cash
when I wanted it, sir, or he would keep the money when I wanted him
to. Why bless you, sir, many's the time when I've been a bit short of
capital when I've gone to Mr. Leslie and said to him that I knew where
I could get some books which I thought might interest him, but that I
was short of the ready cash to finish the deal. Mr. Leslie, sir, he didn't
hesitate. He'd just say, 'How much do you want, Mr. Read?' I'd tell
him and he'd sit down and write me a cheque. People in the trade trust

me, sir. They know I pay my debts, sir, and I know they know. That's how I get along, sir. That's my business. But, sir, you were asking me about Mr. Leslie, sir, well," he stopped for a moment and seemed to be deep in thought, "he had a niece, sir, a lady by the name of Miss Wright. She used to keep house for him, sir. She was an odd old girl, sir, dressed in the fashions of long ago, sir. And I think, sir, that Mr. Leslie must have found her difficult to live with. I remember being in his shop one day, sir, when she started objecting to the dust that was lying about. I must admit, sir, that the shop was rather dusty. But Mr. Leslie, sir, he didn't take it that way, as a piece of well meant criticism and an offer to clear up. No, he said, 'Alice I never interfere with your running of the house, and I'll thank you not to interfere with my business.' I must say, sir, that I thought he was rather harsh to the poor lady. She looked very upset. But then, sir, you must understand that Mr. Leslie was a man who knew his own mind and he couldn't bear to be crossed. I've seen someone in his shop try to beat him down over the price of a book and Mr. Leslie practically ran him out of the shop and told him not to come back, for he wouldn't serve him. But then, sir, I must say that Mr. Leslie was in the right. He knew he was asking a fair price for the book, and that he was making a fair profit. He wasn't one of those who shoved their prices up during the war and spoilt their relationships with their customers. No, sir, Mr. Leslie was a man who knew what he was up to. He kept most of his customers. He would let some of them have almost unlimited credit. He knew which ones he could rely on to pay up in the end. He said he never lost by it."

Mr. Ellis Read seemed to be prepared to go on chattering for hours on end. He sat perched on his shooting-stick like some figure out of a nineteenth century *Punch*. He was as cheerful as a cricket, and his chirp was rather like a cricket's.

The Professor moved awkwardly on top of the pile of bound art magazines and the whole lot slid to the floor with a resounding crash. The old man sat among the wreckage with a faintly bewildered look on his face, as if the ceiling had fallen in on him. He looked suspiciously round the room, at each of us in turn but, finally convinced that none of us had caused the cataclysm, he grinned. Ellis Read helped him to his feet and restored the bundle to its former shape. The old man did not sit down again. He turned to Read.

"Umph," he growled, "Mr. Read, what d'ye know o' Mary Gray?"

Chapter 15

Call Out the Coppers

READ LOOKED at him. He appeared to be honestly surprised.

"Mr. Gray's wife, sir?" he asked. "Ah, there now, sir, you've got a nice lady. She's one in a thousand, sir. There's hardly a time, sir, that I go into that office when she doesn't say, 'How about a nice cup of tea, Mr. Read?' She's a real lady, she is, sir. Why do you want to know, sir? You're not thinking, sir, that she could have had anything to do with the murders, are you?"

"No, son, don't you take on so," the old man was placatory. "I just wanted to know what ye thought o' her. It's wonderful the way ye people always pick a man up when he makes a kinda honest enquiry. It's as though ye thought there was some hidden meanin' in everythin' I say. I tell ye there ain't. I'm as simple minded as the next person, an' I just like to know what people think o' one another. That's all."

He sounded aggrieved. What with the indignity of his fall to the ground, where I realised his weight had done some damage to the rotten floor boards, and people suspecting him of overt motives, the Professor felt that he had every right to feel peeved with the world.

He continued to complain bitterly. From his plaints one would have thought he was an honest hard working botanist, with murder as far from his thoughts as plumbing. Actually, I could see he was enjoying himself enormously. He was nursing some secret to himself. I didn't believe him when he had told me earlier that he knew the name of the murderer. Only too often in the past he had picked his winner with a pin, all but put his shirt on it and then changed horses at the post. The trouble was that the horse he changed to usually won.

Finally we climbed out of Ellis Read's basement, clambering over immense paintings by Benjamin West and Herring, and weaving our way between heaps of books, covered with dust. Read remained affable and friendly. It was obvious that he wanted to help us, but though he was willing to continue talking till the sun went down I did not think we would get any more from him.

The Chief Inspector climbed up the stairs and I followed him. The old man turned round and said something to Read in a low voice. I missed the question but I got the answer. "Never, sir."

The Professor lumbered up on to the pavement, blowing like an aged whale. The Chief Inspector turned to him suspiciously, "What was that you asked Read, John?"

"Oh, nothing, nothing," the Professor was airily off-hand. The Bishop made a gesture of returning to Read's door. The old man scowled at him.

"If you must know," he said bitterly, "and if I can't keep any secrets to myself I was asking Read a question about blunt instruments. Max here can turn round when ye're questionin' a suspect an' buy himself a print o' *The Night-Blowin' Cereus*, an' ye pay no attention to him, but if I as much as look round to ha' a drink, ye immediately jump to the conclusion that I'm hidin' somethin' an' that I got some plot afoot. Bah! All I was askin' him was a question about blunt instruments. Yah!"

"What do you want to know about blunt instruments for?" the Chief Inspector asked with surprise. "If you cast your mind back you'll remember that the doctor said that both blows might have been caused by that shillelagh, the one that was lying in the back of Leslie's shop. Of course, the trouble with these blunt instrument crimes is that they can so rarely be definitely stated to have been done with this or that weapon. On the other hand, John, when you find a weapon that could have been used lying about the scene of the crime you have a pretty fair indication that that was indeed the weapon that was used. What are you going haring about after other weapons for?'

"I ha' me reasons," the old man was stuffily dignified, "an' I'll tell ye them all in due course. Now, if ye'll keep yer nose out o' me business I'd like to make use of the vast resources o' our up-to-date an' competent police-force."

The Chief Inspector looked at him doubtfully.

"Look here, John," he said, "you know I can't just turn the police-force over to you for the fun of it. I've got to know what you want."

"All I want," the old man's voice was mild, "is to be introduced to one o' yer fellers who knows about shops in Central London. You know the sort o' place, a shop where they sell sticks and umbrellas, the sort o' shop where someone might ha' bought somethin' like that

shillelagh. An' then I want a man who can go round the shops askin'
questions for me."

"But look here, John," the Chief Inspector protested, "that shillelagh
was obviously an old second-hand one. It might have been bought at
any junk-shop between here and Land's End. Damn it, man, you can't
expect me to authorise the expenditure of the taxpayer's money on any
wild-goose chase that you happen to think of."

"Hell, son," the old man was getting angry, "I'm a taxpayer, ain't I?
I pay ye an' the rest o' the coppers. I get nothin' back out o't but a
dumb refusal to co-operate. I didn't say I was lookin' for that shillelagh
did I ? Ye can keep me next year's taxes apart an' use 'em to pay for
the copper I want for a couple o' hours. I don't mind. I got me rights
as a British citizen an' as a taxpayer. Dammit, man, it ain't as though I
was askin' you to go crawlin' around the West End on your great belly.
All I want's a copper for a couple o' hours."

"All right, John," the Chief Inspector was weary, "you can have
your copper for a couple of hours, and all I pray is that you don't get
up to too much mischief for I'll have to take the responsibility myself."

"Mind you," the old man was triumphant but suspicious, "I don't
want ye crawlin' around behind me back an' goin to me copper an'
sayin' what was the ole man up to? I'll tell ye soon enough an' I'll gi'ee
me personal word that I won't ask yer peeler to do anythin' which he
be ashamed to tell either his mother or the Commissioner about. Is that
a bargain?"

He blew fiercely at the Chief Inspector through his bushy grey
moustache. He glared over the tops of his glasses, beneath the fringe of
thick grey eyebrows.

The Bishop looked as bland and sleepy as a summer sea.

"You can have it your own way, John," he said comfortably, "so
long as you don't haul me into any trouble on your behalf." His voice
grew meditative. "You know, John, I must say that sometimes I dream
of the day when I'll see you in the dock at the Old Bailey. It will rec-
ompense me for all the disturbance you have caused in my life. I'm a
plain and simple man an' like young Max here all I want is a quiet life,
which I never seem to be able to get when you're around."

The Professor snorted furiously.

"Ye can't blame me for yer thunderin' incompetence," he roared,
and people turned in the street to look at him. "How many o' yer
murders which ha' had ye stumped ha' I solved for ye? Umpteen—I
lost count. Ye wait till ye've a difficult case an' then ye come crawlin'

to me an' askin' me to help ye out. Ye just wait. One o' these days I won't come to yer beck an' call. Ye'll whistle in vain."

This was a fantasy which the old man liked to indulge in. He liked to think that the Bishop came running to him for help, when, as a matter of fact, the affair was exactly the other way round. If there was a murder which appeared the least out of the ordinary no power on earth could have kept John Stubbs away from it, he ran to it like a cat to valerian.

We climbed back into the Bentley and roared off. In the car conversation is, perhaps fortunately, quite impossible. When we arrived at the Yard, the Professor was disgusted to find that Sergeant Graves, the authority on shops, had gone out to lunch. I must say that my sympathies lay entirely with the Sergeant. I was feeling pretty peckish myself. It had been a long morning. I managed to persuade the old man that a little solid food was sometimes good for the stomach. He would have been quite content to vanish into a pub and knock back innumerable pints of beer until the Sergeant returned from lunch.

After we had eaten our lunch, or rather I had eaten mine and the Professor had drunk his, we returned to the Yard. I discovered, to my chagrin, that I was not to be a recipient of his secret. The old man went to closet himself with Sergeant Graves and I pushed off in a huff.

I thought I would go back to Hampstead and get on with some work, but, I must confess, the idea did not appeal to me much. I was on the point of going into David Low's bookshop in Cecil Court to collect the bundle of books I had left there on the afternoon of the murders, when I suddenly remembered the pile of books I had made in old Leslie's shop.

When I remembered these books I remembered also that Miss Wright had been visiting the Chief Inspector for permission to start winding up her uncle's estate. I didn't want these books to be wound up in the estate, so I decided I'd go and call on the old bird. At least it would be a restful afternoon, full of old world courtesy and the feeling that, after all, there were some unalterable values.

I popped down the underground at Leicester Square and took a ticket to Streatham. It didn't occur to me till I was approaching her house that Miss Wright might not be in. It was all right, however. When I rang the bell and listened intently I heard the faint jangle of her chatelaine as she approached the door.

"Good afternoon, Mr. Boyle," she said, "it is nice of you to call on me."

I didn't quite know how to start the ball rolling so I followed her into the drawing-room. It was a bit early for tea but she insisted that a cup of tea would not be amiss.

She left me alone in the room, alone with the stands holding glass bells full of wax fruit and small stuffed birds. The mantelpiece was surmounted by a portrait which looked like a photograph, of a heavily moustached man, his face flanked with wispy whiskers, in the uniform of some regiment of nineteenth century Volunteers. This family portrait was flanked on the left by a steel-engraving of Landseer's *Monarch of the Glen*, and on the right by a chromolithograph of G. F. Watts's *Hope*, a dim figure, a long way after the Italians, sitting in an attitude of the utmost coy despair on the top of a globe, swathed in fluffy clouds. The clock on the mantelpiece was of dark green marble and was surmounted by a bronze sculpture of Perseus rescuing Andromeda—this piece of sculpture looked as though it was the sort of thing which would have won a prize at the Crystal Palace in 1852; no doubt some contemporary gossip had described it as "a highly poetical work"; to my simple mind it was far more obscene than the drawings which Gray had shown us.

The fire-place itself did not fit in with the solid Victorianism of the furnishings of the room. It was in the style of the end of the century, *Art Nouveau*, with arabesques of water-lilies and vine tendrils crawling hopelessly over the highly burnished copper.

The light in the room was softened down to an almost unbearable extent by heavy and elaborate lace curtains.

Miss Wright reappeared. If I had been asked to guess I would have wagered that tea would be served in a silver teapot. It was. There was also a silver hot-water jug, a silver cream-jug, and a silver sugar bowl with silver sugar tongs. The tray was of heavy mahogany, its nakedness hidden by a lace table-cloth. Miss Wright placed her burden on a small occasional table. She served tea.

"I hope, Miss Wright," I began tentatively, "you won't think it rude of me. I was, as you know, the person who stumbled into the shop to find your uncle and Mr. Baird had been murdered. Before that I had been looking round the outside shop making a small pile of books which I wanted to buy. I know it seems grasping of me, but there were one or two books there which I wanted for my work, and so I wondered whether you could tell me who I should apply to. I gather from Chief Inspector Bishop that you are the executor of your uncle's estate?"

"That is quite right, Mr. Boyle," she made a birdlike duck of her head, "I am my uncle's executor and his heir. You are quite right in assuming that I am the correct person to whom to apply."

"Well; I wondered if you would mind selling me these books. I can't, off hand and without seeing them again, remember what the total value of the books was—somewhere in the region of five pounds I would say at a guess. I will write you a cheque for them if you like and you can fill in the amount at your convenience. I hope you don't think I'm being horribly importunate."

"No, no, Mr. Boyle," she assured me with a quick little nod, "I quite understand. You wish for these books in connection with your work. That is right? And you are afraid that in the natural upheaval consequent upon this most unhappy affair they may get lost?"

I indicated that she had the position right in her mind.

"Well, Mr. Boyle," the old lady refilled my cup, "I would be most pleased if you would accept these books as a present from me. No," she silenced my attempt at a protest, "I am not giving away all my unfortunate uncle's estate. But in your case, I feel I owe you something. That nice Chief Inspector said that you did everything that could be done to save my uncle and Mr. Baird. I would like you to accept these books as a mark of the gratitude of my uncle's only living relative."

I protested weakly that I really had not meant to beg for the books, that I had had no such thoughts in my mind when I called on her. But she was very insistent that I should have the books and very firm in her refusal to accept money for them.

"Mr. Boyle," she said primly, "I am an old lady and my uncle has left me very comfortably off. Not only had he a very large sum of money at the bank and in investments, but in addition he carried a considerable amount of life insurance. I have no relatives for whom to amass more money. You are a young man and, no doubt, the saving of five pounds means considerably more to you than it does to me. You can accept these books as a present with a clear conscience, putting my action down to the eccentricity of an old lady."

I protested that I did not consider her eccentric, but only too generous. She smiled at me and changed the subject. She seemed to be very interested in the Professor and in botany. I gathered that, as a girl, she had made a large collection of pressed flowers. She described walks she and a long dead friend had made in Surrey for the purpose of adding to this collection.

As I rose to go she went to an elaborate desk and opened a drawer from which she took a key.

"This Mr. Boyle," she said, handing it to me, "is the key of my uncle's shop. I hope you will excuse my not accompanying you, but I am an old lady and do not wish to go out again to-day. When you have finished with the key, perhaps you will be good enough to send it back to me, by registered post." I went out feeling that I had indeed spent a pleasantly old-world afternoon, far from the rough and tumble of life with Professor Stubbs.

Chapter 16

Blackmailer's Boudoir

WHEN I got home the old man was sitting in his room. He was puffing away at his pipe and reading Curtis's *Botanical Magazine.*

I laid down my bundle of books on a free part of the table.

"What you got there?" he demanded gruffly, and I told him the story of my afternoon. I said that I hoped that he had had as much luck in his pursuits.

He refused to be drawn. I know that when the old man is in his mysterious frame of mind, hiding a head full of secrets, that nothing I can do or say will draw an answer from him. He will talk on any other subject I like but not on the one which I wish to talk about.

I shewed him my treasures and he was interested and informative. I sometimes wonder how he manages to carry so much odd information in his head. After I had taken my books up to my room and had arranged them on the shelves, I went downstairs again.

The old man was seated at his desk. He was making notes which were gathering round him like leaves round the foot of a tree in autumn. I picked up a handful of these notes and gave a mental groan.

Professor Stubbs was engaged on his long overdue *History of Botany.* I knew that I was in for a long evening of filing and arranging. I kept a special filing cabinet for these notes, and every time the old man added to them I had to add to a most elaborate cross-index which I had been forced to compile.

It was a long evening. It lasted till two-thirty when I pushed off to bed leaving the Professor still hard at work, converging scraps of paper with notes in his minute and legible hand. I had to rush all round the house finding books as he wanted them.

When I had first started to live with the Professor I had tried to instal some system into the bookshelves. I had arranged them under different headings and under authors. I had long ago given up the struggle. I still tried to keep the books on the shelves, but I no longer worried when

I found a detective story sandwiched between the volumes of the ency-clopaedia. It would have made my life a hell on earth if I had really worried about these things.

Books which should have been on the shelves in the old man's room had somehow wandered into my rooms or into his bedroom.

When I wandered down to breakfast I found the old man was already up. He was swathed in an immense tartan dressing-gown and his pipe was going full blast. He had done the necessary chores, attend-ing to the plants which had filtered from the garden into the house and so on.

We breakfast rather late, at about half-past nine. This lets us get a certain amount of work done first and I think it is a good idea. Over breakfast the old man was not communicative. He was perfectly willing to speak about the notes he had been making for his *History of Botany* but he wouldn't discuss the case at all. He seemed to be nursing some secret which was pleasing him and he was unwilling to let anyone else have a share of it.

I bickered with him mildly about this. We always bicker over break-fast. It takes the sting out of the day.

After breakfast, he dressed quickly. I did not know whether I was in on the day's outing so I said nothing. I sat down at a table and tried to arrange the notes which had gathered after I had gone to bed. Judging from the number of them I would say that the old man hadn't been to bed at all.

I was playing dignified silence. I did not want any piece of his mur-ders. When he came into the room ready dressed to go out, I put on my most innocent air.

"Going out, sir?" I asked rather obviously, "is there anything I can do for you till you come back?"

"Ain't ye comin' wi' me, Max?" he asked with an expression of surprise. "I kinda thought o' takin' a look at Baird's flat. I got permis-sion from the Bishop to go there an' I wondered what kinda establish-ment a blackmailer keeps up."

Mr. Cecil Baird had certainly believed in comfort. He had a large flat in one of those blocks off Park Lane. The furniture was expensive and comfortable, and it appeared to have been chosen with considerable taste. On one wall I noticed the Augustus John drawing which Gray had spoken about. It was a good one, a damned good one.

The old man lumbered about the flat with the noise of a herd of elephants crashing through the jungle. I missed the noise and went in search of him. He was perched on the edge of the late Mr. Baird's bed. A glass-fronted bookshelf beside the bed looked as though it had been broken open. There was a suggestive splintering of the wood round the lock.

"Did you do this?" I asked sternly.

"Why yes," the old man looked up at me with a face of innocence. "I just kinda wanted to see what kinda litratoor a blackmailer had on his shelves. Considerin' he was so dam' upright an' was so thunderin' upset about other people's lapses from the straight an' narrow that he made 'em pay for it, Mr. Baird went in for an odd kinda book. Look at 'em."

I looked at them. So far as I could see they were the ordinary run of pornography, copies of Sade bound in expensive morocco, several German books of erotic photographs and that book which must be most disappointing to those who want obscenity, Lawrence's *Lady Chatterly's Lover*.

"I suppose he got these from Leslie," I said, "I wonder if Leslie's name was among those ticked off in his note-book?" The old man dug at his hair with a blunt thumb. I think he had forgotten that he was wearing that lunatic hat, for it fell off and rolled under the bed. He left it there. It seemed he felt more comfortable with his hair loose. He tousled it wildly.

"Dam' me," he grunted, "that's somethin' I forgot to ask the Bishop. Be a good lad, Max, an' ring him up an' ask him about it."

I thought of telling him to do his own phoning. He approaches the telephone like a man about to grapple with a snake which may, or may not be poisonous. He gets his number by the simple expedient of ringing up the exchange and demanding that they get it for him. I don't think he has ever quite mastered the dial system. He'd be furious if he knew I thought this as he is always insisting that he has a mechanical mind. He certainly is fond of gadgets, but it is a fondness which I rather deprecate. All mechanical gadgets are only too apt to become sticks to beat my back. I have to take them to pieces and explain how they work. What's worse is that I have to put them together again and mend them whenever the old man does something to them that makes them go wrong.

I decided that I would play ball with him and went over to the telephone in the sitting room.

The Bishop was in. After some delay I got through to him. He then had to find the little black note-book. It was in some other department where they were trying to tie up the names in it with real people, so that they could know a bit more about Mr. Baird's very extensive activities as a blackmailer.

Finally, however, I got my answer. No, Leslie's name had not got a tick against it. It was there all right, but was, like so many more, not ticked off.

I went and delivered this message to the old man. His nose was stuck deep into the pages of one of the books of erotic photographs. He was not abashed.

"Dirty little boy," I said rudely.

"What, me, Max?" he said in astonishment, "eh? I find these photographs thunderin' funny. Just look at this one."

My vaguely puritan ancestry made me feel that I was indeed being very wicked as I joined him in looking through the book. However, I had to confess that on the whole the photographs were more amusing and astonishing than pornographic.

Finally the old man laid the book down. He stuck his pipe in his mouth and glowered at the ceiling.

Suddenly he slapped his hand down on his knees with a resounding crack.

"Got it," he roared triumphantly, "these ticks against names ha' bin worryin' me all along. Why, if Baird was a professional blackmailer, was there only one tick against each name ? Ye'd expect to find a dozen or more against every one. It wasn't as if the note book was a new one into which he seemed to ha' transferred his list o' accounts. Some o' the names seemed to ha' bin there for a long time."

I didn't know what he was burbling about.

"I suppose," I said helpfully, "that that little note-book represented Baird's list of victims. It was a kind of ledger, the book in which he kept the names of his customers, so as to speak."

"That's just it, Max," the old man growled at me, "supposin' that little book was Baird's private list o' his victims, why did he suddenly start puttin' ticks against their names, eh?"

I didn't know and I said so. I said that it was difficult for me to enter the mind of a blackmailer, as it wasn't the sort of mind that I could understand. I could understand, say, Charles Hume or Bert Gorman. They were ordinary honest thieves, but Baird was beyond me.

The Professor ignored my remarks. He took out his immense flame-throwing petrol-lighter and applied its flare to his pipe. Once he was comfortably surrounded with clouds of nauseous smoke, he leaned back on the bed and grinned at me. He certainly seemed to be very pleased with himself. I scowled at him. I just couldn't see what he was driving at.

"Uhhuh," he rumbled, "Well, now, supposin' that Baird was in the process o' windin' up his business as a blackmailer. He wasn't the sort o' man who'd just disappear an' leave his victims be. Not him. He'd think that, if he was foldin' the profession up, he might as well make a killin' on each victim. Say he went round to each o' 'em an' said, 'Look'ee here, I'm kinda reformed character. I'm kinda gettin' out o' this dirty profession, an' I thought I'd be decent an' offer ye the proof which I ha' bin usin' against ye. Naturally, as I'm a poor man I can't do this for nothin', but tell ye what I'll do. I bin gettin' a tenner a month from ye. Well, I'll let ye have the proof which I hold against ye for five hundred quid. What d'ye say to that, Max? If ye'd been in the position o' one o' Baird's victims, ye'd ha' bin only too pleased to help buy him out o' business. It would be cheaper in the long run, an' ye'd feel the whale o' a lot safer once ye'd lit the kitchen stove wi' the damnin' evidence, wouldn't ye?"

I agreed. It seemed to me that the old man certainly had something there. The only trouble was that I could not see what immediate bearing it had on the murders.

"Hum," the old man growled to himself, "Humm, the next thin' we got to do is to find out if Baird was thinkin' o' leavin' the country, eh?"

He rose to his feet and went lumbering round the flat once more. He came to a halt before a strongly built desk. The top was closed and locked. He looked at it speculatively.

"I'm just wonderin'," he mumbled, "if Baird's passport is hidden in here. If we could find that it might give us some kinda indication o' his intentions about the immediate future.

The immediate future, that is, that he was plannin' when he met wi' his overdue death."

He was fishing through his pockets as he spoke. He took out a bunch of keys and a large strong Norwegian knife. He tried the keys in the lock, one after the other, but none of them made the least impression. With an expression of devilish glee the old man opened the knife.

I had the hell of a job preventing him breaking open the desk. His earlier successful experiment with the bookcase beside the bed seemed to have given him a taste for destruction. He protested bitterly that he was sure that he would have made a good house-breaker, but in the end I had my own way.

I went to the telephone and again made contact with the Chief Inspector. The old man took the phone from me once I got through.

"Hey, Reggie," he bellowed into the mouthpiece, "It's me, John Stubbs. I just kinda wanted to know if Baird had a passport. Yes I kinda got an idea that he was windin' up his business an' was goin' round his victims makin' a final killin'. Well, you find out for me. Ring me back here. I'll wait. I'm havin' the dickens o' a good time lookin' through Mr. Baird's collection o' comic photos. Ye should just see 'em sometime. No, no, Reggie, I ain't breakin' the house down. I ain't done any damage to speak o'. Try the blinkin' Foreign Office an' see if they can tell ye whether Baird had applied for a passport recently. No, no, Max is here wi' me an' he'll vouch for me. He'll swear I ain't breakin' the house down. What's that ye say? Eh? Bah!"He slammed down the telephone, and turned an injured face towards me.

"Suspicious lot o' hounds," he grumbled, "always thinkin' I'm breakin' thin's up. Blinkin' Reggie has the dam' nerve to say that he hopes that ye're keepin' me out o' mischief. Bah! before I know where I am I'll be goin' around wi' a blinkin' keeper. Thunderin' lot o' fools, they ought to know by this time that I'm not in the habit o' smashin' thin's."

I walked slowly through to the next room and looked at the damaged bookcase. The old man wandered heavily after me, sniffing suspiciously. I looked pointedly at the frayed wood but said nothing.

"Dammit all," he exploded, "I wanted to get a book out o' that case an' none o' me keys would fit the lock so I dam' well just had to break in. It is not as though I was in the habit o' doin' wanton damage. I only break into thin's that would give way to gentle persuasion. Anyhow, I only kinda coaxed that door open wi' the blade o' me knife. I didn't force it."

He continued grumbling for quite a time. Anyone would have thought that he was the most misjudged and injured person in London. He gave the impression that he could not move without people trying to interfere with him. He worked himself up into quite a rage.

The telephone shrilled and he advanced towards it with such an air of determination that I feared he was about to pull it out by its roots.

He yanked the receiver off with considerable vigour and put it to his face.

"Yes," he bellowed furiously, "it's me. Yes, dammit, it's Stubbs. Yes. Yes. Thank'ee."

He bashed the receiver back into its cradle and turned to me. His bad temper had vanished like a thunder-cloud before the sun.

"I was right," he boomed triumphantly, "Mr. Cecil Baird had applied to ha' his passport renewed a fortnight ago. I dunno what Reggie did to the thunderin' Foreign Office but he certainly got his reply quick."

Chapter 17

Insight on Uncle

ALL THE same, I must say I didn't see where this information was going to lead us. Perhaps Mr. Cecil Baird might have been engaged in the preliminaries to his retirement. Well, and that was that. I couldn't understand where this new information tied up with the murders.

I asked the Professor but he played mysterious. I was annoyed. I did all the donkey work, it seemed to me, and he refused to share the results of my work with me. I felt I was being pretty hardly dealt with. I said so, at considerable length, over lunch. It was a good lunch.

We were swilling brandy in the smoking room of the Professor's club after we had finished lunch when I put my hand in my pocket. I was looking for a match. My cigar had gone out. I found Miss Wright's key.

I had forgotten to post it back to her. I got up slowly and told the old man that I had to go and buy a registered envelope.

"Why not," he said, "deliver the key in person an' take the opportunity o' thankin' the old lady for the books now ye've had a chance to look at 'em? She's the kinda old lady who'd appreciate that as a politeness."

I agreed. I didn't know what the old man was holding up his sleeve. Sometimes I think he pretends he's got a straight flush when there's nothing there but his arm.

I was just about to start out to go by Underground when the Professor sat upright in his chair.

"Tell ye what," he announced, "I'll run ye down in the car. Maybe the old lady'll gi'us a cup o' tea. Anyhow I got one or two questions I'd like to ask her. Ones I kinda forgot the other day."

Every now and again I swear a solemn oath that I will never travel in that damn Bentley again. At least, not when the Professor's driving. I must be pretty weak willed where the old man is concerned. I climbed up into the car like a lamb ready for the slaughter. This is a true description of the old man's driving. Every time I sit in that car I feel I am a plump lamb waiting to be sacrificed to some odd god or other, Moloch or Mercury, it doesn't matter which. The Professor's driving would curl the hairs of a Russian ballet dancer. It would have turned a Skye terrier into an Aberdeen. What it did to me was nobody's business. All I can say is that I've been frightened enough in my time, but nothing frightens me quite so much as the old man at the wheel.

Miss Wright welcomed us with charming smiles. She seemed to be genuinely pleased to see us. She sat us down among the Victorian bric-a-brac and left to prepare a cup of tea. I noticed her tea was China tea. She told me that she went up to Piccadilly once a month and bought it from Jacksons. It was *Earl Grey* tea. Neither she nor her uncle had ever been able to stand any other and she praised Jacksons for the fact that even during the war they had made serious efforts to keep up the quality of the tea.

She asked the old man a great number of questions about botany. Her approach to the subject was that of the late Victorian lady. The name of Mendel was a cipher to her. I was amused to hear the old man trying to explain the theory of genetics in simple words.

"Well, ma'am," he was saying, "say ye got two peas an' one of em's wrinkled an' t'other's plain, and ye breed 'em together. Well, ye kinda get a regular pattern in their descendants. Like this, ye see."

He dug one of his stubs of pencil from his pocket and proceeded to demonstrate on the back of an envelope which I passed him. He had, it seemed to me, been preparing to jot his little symbols on the linen and lace cloth which covered the tray.

Suddenly, having given a fair outline of the theory of inheritance, the old man switched the subject.

"Ma'am," he growled, "as ye may know we bin lookin' into the matter o' yer uncle's death. There's still one or two things which kinda worry us. One of 'em is we don't know enough about his connection wi' Cecil Baird. Has anythin' occurred to ye that ye think we should know?"

Miss Wright looked round her drawing room. She eyed the stuffed green budgerigars with pleasure and her gentle eyes doted on the Watts beside the mantelpiece. She seemed to be thinking of these things and not of the question which the Professor had put to her.

She came back from her Cook's tour of the pleasures of her room and sighed.

"Mr. Baird, Professor," she said slowly, "was not at all a nice man. He was a horrible man. It is a good thing that he is dead. I have never before said that about anyone, but I'll say it again about Mr. Baird. It's a very good thing that he is dead. He caused a lot of people a great deal of unhappiness." Her voice was unexpectedly vehement. "He was a wicked, wicked man, who made a living out of other people's frailties. We all have our family skeletons. Well, this horrible Mr. Baird made it his business to find out about people's family skeletons and then he went on to ask for money for keeping quiet about them. He was what I believe is called a blackmailer. He should have been sent to prison."

The Professor was chewing at his empty pipe. I could see that he wanted to smoke, but that even he felt that his tobacco would be out of place in the cloistered half-light of Miss Wright's drawing-room.

"Do smoke if you want to, Professor," she smiled at him gently, "I am quite used to strong tobacco. My uncle used to smoke little black cheroots. As I was saying, Mr. Baird was a nasty wicked man. I know that it has been discovered that Uncle Allan was not always honest in the things that he handled, but he was a saint beside Mr. Baird. Mr. Baird was blackmailing my uncle."

She made this last statement without the slightest alteration in tone. The old man, who had got his pipe alight, looked out at her from the smoke around his face.

"Uhhuh, ma'am," he grunted, "an' how d'ye know that?"

"I have every reason to know it," she replied softly, "I had noticed that whenever Mr. Baird came near him Uncle Allan bristled like a dog that is about to fight with another dog. Baird used to ring him up about once a month and then he would come round and see uncle. They would be shut up together in Uncle's room for about half an hour. After Mr. Baird's visits Uncle Allan was more difficult than usual to deal with. He would sit with a book open on his knees without reading it and he would snap at me if I asked him a simple question, such as what he would like for supper or whether he intended to have a bath. One night—I don't think he knew I was in the room—I heard him saying to himself something like 'Ten per cent.—ten per cent.—it's an intolerable drain. I can't go on like this.' Then he saw me and he stopped but I could see his mouth still making the shape of the words 'Ten per cent.'"

She paused to offer us more tea, which she poured delicately into thin nineteenth century tea cups. She passed round the silver sugar bowl and the silver cream jug.

"That," she went on, "was all I knew about Mr. Baird's relations with my uncle. I didn't then even know that he was being blackmailed. I had no reason to think that there was anything wrong about Uncle

Allan's business. That is, I mean that so far as I knew it was a quite ordinary bookselling business and that he made enough by it to enable him to live very comfortably. It was only last night that I found some papers which shewed me that Mr. Baird had been blackmailing my uncle."

"Uhhuh," the Professor nodded, "can I see these papers? They may have some bearing on the case and may help us to find who it was that murdered your uncle. Y'see it's a matter o' buildin' up the case like a jigsaw puzzle. We got to find all the bits first an' until we ha' enough, we can't tell which bits belong to this puzzle an' which are merely fortuitous pieces o' a much greater puzzle—the puzzle o' human nature."

Miss Wright rose to her feet and, with a small key from her chatelaine unlocked the bureau from which she had taken the key the previous night to give it to me. She took out a long manilla envelope which she handed to the Professor.

I could see, over his shoulder, that it was a used envelope, addressed in an unfamiliar hand to Cecil Baird, Esq. The Professor turned back the flap and slid some papers out into his hand. He unfolded them carefully. Even a quick glance shewed that some of them dealt with the matter of stolen books.

The most damning document, however, was a paper in Allan Leslie's hand, dated nearly three years earlier. It was nothing less than a signed confession that he had been dealing in stolen books over a period of some years. I whistled gently as I read through it.

The old man appeared to be bewildered as he turned the envelope this way and that in his hand.

"You will understand, Professor Stubbs," Miss Wright was prim, "that I would be most grateful if you could treat this information as confidential. Naturally, I want as few people as possible to know about uncle's—er—failings. You see," her voice was faintly appealing, "to most of the people around us, here, he was a very respectable business man. It is bad that he has been murdered, but, you know, I think I will be able to live that down."

I think she caught my eye upon her. She stopped for a moment and took a sip of tea before she went on.

"Mr. Boyle is a very young man, Professor, and perhaps he doesn't yet understand that one can share a home with someone without being really and deeply fond of that person. I respected Uncle Allan and, in a way I suppose, I was fond of him. But there was no bond of real affection between us. I think I felt that he always cared more for books than for human beings. He was always nice to me, but never shewed me any affection. He was inclined to be mean about housekeeping things, too. However, I was very happy living with him. I was mistress of this house and that means a lot to an old lady like myself. I was able to have all my own things around me. All these things," she indicated the furnishings of the drawing-room, "belong to me. I inherited them from my mother who was Uncle Allan's sister. Uncle Allan's death was certainly a shock to me, a very severe shock, but I cannot truthfully say that it broke my heart. In my generation we were brought up to hide our feelings, but it sometimes seems to me that the modern attitude of accepting things like that and bringing them out into the open is much to be preferred. I was taught to be honest and so I feel that there is no point in my disguising my feelings about Uncle Allan. He was in a way very very difficult. He could not brook what he called interference. He would always have his own way about everything. Perhaps the most annoying thing about him was that he was always right. No matter what went wrong it was someone else's fault. If he got up late in the morning it was either the maid's fault or mine. I don't blame him for this, as I knew my mother and from her I had often heard that Uncle Allan was a spoiled child, one who always had his own way."

She took another sip of tea. There was a faint rosy flush on the temples below the grey hair.

"Mother died," she went on, "just after Uncle Allan's wife had left him. She got a divorce and is now somewhere in America. Having lived with my uncle for all these years I am probably prejudiced in his wife's favour. I can understand exactly why she left him. She was a beautiful girl, high spirited and full of affection. To be honest I have to confess that she must have found uncle what they call a 'dry old stick.'" She looked round us with a pert look of enquiry, as if to ask whether she had got the phrase correcdy.

I noticed that the Professor was still holding the papers that she had given him in his hand. He leaned forward and looked at her.

"I wonder, ma'am," he rumbled politely, "if ye'd tell me where ye found these papers. The police did a fairly thorough search of the house an' they didn't stumble on them."

"Oh," she said, "I was clearing up the house. You know I was trying to make the place look as I have always wanted it to look and I came across them somewhere or other. Let me think," she creased her brows in concentration, "oh, I know where it was. When you came into the house did you notice a large Chinese pot in the hall?" I nodded politely. I had noticed the pot. It was a horror. "Well, that pot belonged to my mother. She always kept it filled with bulrushes all winter." She hesitated and looked at the Professor. The botany she had learnt in her youth was coming back to her. "At least," she went on, "mother and I always called them bulrushes though I believe that they are really called royal rushes?"

She turned towards the Professor for correction. He smiled at her, a gargantuan beam of good feeling.

"Anyhow," she said, "that doesn't really matter. But when I came to live with uncle he said he couldn't stand the sight of it. He insisted that I should keep it in the hall. He used to stick his umbrella into it when he came home on wet nights. I must admit," her voice was shy, "that this habit of his was one that grated on me. Well, when I was clearing up after his decease, I thought I would put the pot in my bedroom. It is there now, filled with pampas grass and it looks very pretty. Very pretty indeed. Naturally, when I moved it I washed it out. You have no idea how much dirt had accumulated from his habit of putting his wet umbrella into it. It was in the bottom of this jar that I found the envelope full of these papers. I was just about to throw it away when I thought that the police might be angry with me if I did that as they had asked me to give them any information that I could. I nearly told Mr. Boyle about it yesterday afternoon, but somehow I couldn't quite bring myself to do it. Uncle's reputation has suffered enough from the stories that have been going round. I thought this morning that I would burn the papers unless someone asked me about them within twenty-four hours."

She looked round at us anxiously. She was fingering a string of heavy amber and Whitby jet beads at her throat The old man made an encouraging noise, the sort of noise that a chap makes when he is calling chickens in to feed them, Miss Wright interpreted the sound correctly.

"So you see, Professor," she said simply, "when you asked me for the papers—did you guess that there were such papers? You solved my problem for me. I gave them to you and my conscience is clear."

Chapter 18

Case Going Begging

IT SEEMED to me that we were pinning our whole faith to the idea that the murders had been done by an associate of Allan Leslie, when they might just as well have been done by any one of the people mentioned in Baird's note-book. In fact it seemed that it was almost certainly one of these people who had done the murders and not anyone connected with Leslie.

After all, so far as I could see, no one had any real reason for murdering Leslie, but the devil of a large number had every reason for wishing to see Baird safely in his grave, provided that by doing so they did not either run their necks into a noose or give away the things which he had been blackmailing them about.

Perhaps the unfortunate Leslie had been the victim of a chain of circumstances which had necessitated his death.

I said all this to Professor Stubbs. He looked up from his book and took a swig of beer. He nodded his head.

"Uhhuh," he growled, "I thought o' that. But can ye tell me o' any person who'd risk murderin' Baird if they knew he still had the stuff he was blackmailin' 'em wi', eh? An' now we decided that he was closin' the business, who was goin' to risk shovin' their head into a dam' noose for the sake o' revenge. Revenge may read all very well as the motive for murder in a tuppenny-ha'penny thriller, but in real life, ye'll find that most people are more concerned wi' the safety o' their own skins than wi' makin' their oppressors squirm. Once ye had the evidence which Baird had collected against ye, ye'd burn the dam' stuff an' say good riddance to the thunderin' pest—ye might hope he'd get malaria an' die o't abroad, but ye wouldn't go out an' kill him. Ye'd no longer ha' any real reason for that, eh?"

I saw the old man's point that time. It was quite true that no one who was being blackmailed by him would dare kill him—unless of course by so doing they were making certain that they obtained the damning evidence at the same time—and, on the other hand, if he really was intending to retire, there was no reason for anyone who had paid for the last time to murder Baird.

"As for yer other point," the old man went on, "that Baird was to be the victim o' the murder. Well, if ye'll think for a moment ye'll see that the murderer knew all about Leslie's shop. The murderer knew that the door had an outside bolt, and also knew that the gas ring was faulty, an' only worked when someone fed the gas wi' coppers. If ye remember, Miss Wright said she'd bin naggin' at her uncle to buy another for a long time, but, bein' the sort o' man he was, the fact that his niece wanted him to buy a gas-ring in workin' order was the one thin' that would ha' made him postpone the purchase o' one. He seems to ha' bin the sort o' feller who might be on his way out to buy a new one, and on someone approvin' o' his action, he would immediately drop the idea. Anythin' like that came under the headin' o' interference to him."

"Are the police gettin' on very well with the names in Baird's note-book?" I wanted to know.

"Bah!" the Professor snorted, "as well as ye can expect them to get on in a case o' blackmail. Most o' the names that have been traced ha' firmly denied that Baird was anythin' more than an acquaintance. A copper says to 'em, 'Ye're quite sure that Baird wasn't blackmailin' ye?' An' they look at him as if he'd belched in church, 'Blackmail,' they says, 'blackmail? What's that? What would Mr. Baird ha' had to black-mail me about? I never done anythin' wrong.' Bah! The police are findin' an overwhelmin' lack o' cooperation. An', yet, ye know, ye can't really blame 'em. So long as they ain't done anythin' really crimi-nal, the police won't pay any attention to it, but all the same they feel it's better to play Brer Rabbit about the whole affair."

I had managed to get the old man going and thought I might get some more information out of him.

"Well," I said cheerfully in an off-hand manner, "it seems that we're stumped. We don't know who did the murder nor why it was done. For, in spite of his dealing in stolen books and pornography, no one seems to have had any real reason for killing Leslie."

"Uhhuh," he said and his eyes twinkled wickedly through the gap between the tops of his steel-rimmed glasses and his bushy grey eye-brows. "I know who done it, an' I think I can guess why. Ye must try an' work it out for yerself. It was someone who knew Leslie well, mind ye."

I set to work. I made a list of all the people we had seen in connection with Leslie and Baird. I still couldn't get the answer. A lot of obstruction seemed to me to be the trouble with the case. If, as I gathered the old man had meant, Leslie was the primary victim, then I could see no reason for murdering him. In addition the murder of Baird along with him, considered as a fortuitous action, had been the cause of our running around looking into innumerable mares' nests and smelling after uncounted red-herrings. In fact, we had, it seemed to me, been dancing up a lot of garden-paths and barking up many wrong trees. If I kept on at this rate I felt I would mix enough metaphors to make a verbal haggis.

I started to reconsider the cases against Ellis Read and Henry Gray. The trouble was that I liked them both and I could not manage to dissociate my liking from my suspicions.

Neither of them had an alibi.

To consider Read first. He was an odd little man, who might easily have been said to know far too much. He was a veritable store-house of information on the subject of picture dealing and bookselling. No doubt someone like Leslie or Hume might very well have wanted to murder him as a potential danger to their illicit concerns, but, on the other hand, I couldn't see him murdering anyone.

I realised that, although Read seemed to have talked a great deal, he had done no more than answer our questions. He had larded his conversation liberally with references to his business, but had not supplied much information about that business. It seemed that, under cover of this flow of verbiage, Read knew how to keep his own council. He had not, finally told us much that we would not have found out for ourselves.

Certainly he had put the Chief Inspector on to Bert Gorman. But, from what Gorman had said, it seemed that he would have come along and given himself up of his own accord sooner or later, to try and clear himself of the suspicion of being mixed up in a murder case. All Read had done was to expedite matters by a few hours. I felt convinced that he knew far more than he had told us, and that he had only said exactly what suited him. All the same I was forced to admit that I could not cast him for the role of murderer.

Henry Gray, now, was a rather different case. He was as charming as you could wish. I had fallen for that charm. I also envied him his wife, but that had nothing to do with the case. Say, for instance that he had been only telling part of the story when he admitted that he knew

Baird. It did not seem likely that if Baird had known anything really bad he would have been content with one drawing by Augustus John.

Of course, Gray's explanation that he had nothing to fear, but that he considered it easier to let the drawing go than to have all the bother of a police-court, with the possibility of having to enter into long explanations about the obscene drawings, was very reasonable. I tried to put myself in his position and I could see that, if the drawing meant little to me financially, I would most probably have behaved in the same way.

At the same time, however, suppose that Baird had had something really damning on Gray, and had announced that he was willing to settle the whole affair for an outright sum, and had further said that he would come around that afternoon and deliver the evidence in return for the money.

Why, the idea seemed to me to be simple, that would probably explain Gray's action in going round to see Leslie. He wanted to raise cash on the drawings as quickly as possible, and Leslie had a reputation for paying on the spot. When he saw Baird it might have occurred to him that the blackmailer probably had the papers on him and he might have taken the risk of knocking him out and trying to lay his hands on the evidence. That seemed to me to be possible.

The trouble lay in old Leslie. Why was he killed, too? Why had Gray needed to kill Baird? Baird would never have dared to bring an action for assault and once Gray had the papers he was perfectly safe. It wasn't reasonable to suppose that Leslie had come in and found Gray engaged in rifling Baird's body and that Gray had knocked him out too.

No matter if Leslie was irascible, if Gray had explained his action Leslie would probably have been amenable to reason. It seemed probable that as he was also one of Baird's victims he might even have been sympathetic and helpful. To begin with, allowing that Leslie had been out of the shop for a moment, he might have been pretty annoyed to find that Gray was making use of his shop as a prize-ring, but no doubt Gray's charm would have had its effect in due time and he would have been all right.

That took me away on a side-line. I wondered why Baird was visiting Leslie if the latter had already obtained the evidence against him. Why hadn't Baird crossed off Leslie's name on his list? And, again, a large Chinese pot seemed an odd place to hide anything. It was so obvious. Of course, I remembered Poe's *Purloined Letter*, that might be reason for it. All the same, I very much doubted if any detective from

Scotland Yard would have missed the *Purloined Letter* had he started out to look for it.

Say, however—I returned to the problem of Gray—that he had been talking to Leslie and Leslie had let slip that he was expecting Baird. Well, Gray had struck me as a pretty cool card. He might have taken the opportunity of knocking out Leslie and then have lain in wait for Baird.

Baird would perhaps have peered into the back-shop when Leslie did not come out to him and then Gray could have knocked him on the head. Once he had got his papers from Baird's pockets he might have panicked and the rest of the case might have been a result of this panic. All he had to do was to leave the two men lying knocked out on the floor, close and bolt the door behind him, shove a shilling or two in the gas-meter and go off to his news-reel.

This didn't seem to me to be a flawless case against Gray, but it had its points. I wrote out a rough résumé of it on a piece of paper. When I had tidied it up it looked fairly strong. I put it to the old man.

He read my short notes carefully, swilling beer between the sentences.

"Umm, yes," he said slowly, "I see yer case. Ye've tumbled to it, an' so has the Bishop. He's workin' away on the same line so far as I can make out. The trouble is I bin tryin' to keep somethin' up my sleeve. I don't want to move unless I'm forced to."

"What do you mean?" I asked crossly, "You've got something up your sleeve? That's not fair. Damn it all, sir, you yourself object to the detective story where all the cards are not placed properly on the table. Now you're trying to do the same thing yourself."

"No, no, son," I could see he was shocked by my suggestion that he was cheating, "I don't mean I'bin holdin' out on you. Ye know thunderin' well that I wouldn't do that on ye. All I mean is that I drew the correct deduction from a fact that was lyin' there for all o' ye to see, an' that I know who did the murder. I didn't want to have to move. The trouble about the case is that so much o' it was accidental. I got nothin' you ain't got to work on. Me little private business at Scotland Yard this afternoon just kinda had to do wi' me little fact an' me deduction from it."

He sighed heavily. He looked rather unhappy. I could have sworn that his bushy moustache had a sort of droop to it. He hoisted himself out of his chair and lumbered over to the beer barrel in the corner, collecting my pint tankard as he went. He filled the mugs and returned to the chair. He downed about half of his quart and wiped a few bubbles of froth from his moustache. He lit his pipe. All this business took longer than it does to write it down, for with the Professor everything seemed to have its proper ritual. The job of filling tankards was not one that could be done in a hurry, for he liked them full, with just the right amount of head on them. I was not allowed to pour beer for the old man as one day I had joggled the barrel and had made the contents cloudy. This was, I think, the only sin which he had not forgiven me. Anything else was pardonable, but to make beer undrinkable was a very high blasphemy.

He was looking through my sheet of paper again. He frowned at it heavily. The clouds of smoke from his pipe were drifting up to the ceiling above him.

"Uhhuh, Max," he growled, "ye've made yer case. I can start pullin' holes in it, but it might as well lie for the moment. I bin wonderin' when ye'd get round to it. Ye see it stands out a mile that Gray is one o' the people who could ha' done it. All I'll tell ye is that ye're wrong."

I wanted to know where I was wrong, but he wouldn't tell me. He insisted that I had all the facts at my command, and that if he could make them fit together I could. No doubt this was right, but, though I am much better housetrained than the old man, and like things tidy around me, I must admit that my brain is very much less tidy. It always surprises me when I consider the diffuseness of his knowledge that the old man can draw the facts out from the various corners of his brain and put them together so that there are no gaps between them. If I had a brain like that I'd probably stop worrying when I find volumes of Curtis's *Botanical Magazine* taking the place of a hot-water bottle in my bed. I'd be glad to stop worrying about things like that— worrying doesn't do any good—the poltergeist still moves things around the house in an inexplicable way. I'd be glad to have the old man's brain.

"O' course, Max," he went on heavily, "ye're right in one way. Ye try an' tie the two murders together. Ye seem to ha' realised that they are both a part o' the scheme o' things an' that one murder couldn't ha' happened wi'out t'other. In fact I may tell ye that both murders are the result o' a chain o' accidents, an' that no one is more worried about that than the murderer."

"Who is the murderer?" I asked him outright.

He shook his head heavily. He ran his blunt hands through his mop of hair, making it stand round his head like a grey halo, the halo that has not been washed with Persil.

"Um, ye know," he rumbled slowly, "I'd like to leave things as they are if it is possible. T'ain't like me to want to leave a case unfinished, but here I can see no good that can be done by me solvin' it. No one is very much under suspicion, an' unless the police move, thin's 'ull be as well left that way."

Chapter 19

Grumbles at Guilt

THE OLD man dawdled over breakfast. He seemed to be expecting something to happen. I did not say much to him as I was still trying to puzzle out his remarks of the previous night. He sat opposite me, morose in his tartan dressing gown, chewing pieces of toast with a vigour which they did not require. He drank two pint mugs full of coffee.

After he had breakfasted I did the household jobs as quickly as I could, and went round the garden on a tour of inspection, to see that none of the plants were feeling seedy. I did all this thoroughly and quickly, as I expected, from my experience of the last few days, that the old man would want to go out somewhere.

However, when I entered the house I found him, still slumped in his dressing gown, at his desk. He was writing. I did not like to look over his shoulder, so I went on with some of my own work, my real work as a botanist. I was in the middle of a problem which required the most outlandish statistics when I realised that the Professor was looking at me. I looked up at him. He looked helpless and rather worried, like a baby that has suddenly become middle-aged and doesn't know what to do about it.

"Ye know, Max," he grumbled, "it ain't like me, but I just can't seem to concentrate on anythin' this mornin'. I was tryin' to do some work, but I can't keep me mind off this dam' case. I keep on wonderin' if I'm doing right. I don't believe in helpin' murderers, but in this case I don't want to catch the murderer. Ye see, in the ordinary case, if the murderer feels that he or she's suspected they may try an' cover thin's up by committin' a second or a third murder. Here, I may say, I think I'm morally certain that the murderer will do no such thing. The first murders were, as I've said, rather more accidental than intentional, an' the murderer is not one by any instinct to murder. Ye see, this is in a way a case wi'out any real cause."

"I say, sir," I was surprised, "you told me last night that the murders could not have taken place separately, didn't you? And now you are saying that there was no real cause for them. What do you mean?"

"Just exactly what I say," he growled, "the murders are tied together closely, but there was no real cause for them."

I chewed on this. It seemed screwy. Then it dawned on me. I thought I saw what he was getting at.

"You mean," I asked, "that after all this was a murder of revenge? That the murderer had got back the evidence from Baird and yet was determined to kill him? In that case the death of Leslie *was* quite fortuitous."

"No," he looked at me gloomily, "I don't mean anythin' o' the kind. I said all along that I don't think this was a case o' murder for revenge. When ye know the murderer, which is somethin' ye can work out for yerself, ye'll see what I mean, an' ye'll see how the murders were causeless and yet connected. Once ye got that worked out, mabbe ye'll see what I'm drivin' at. Ye'll understand why I don't want to make a move."

He sighed heavily and swung round to his desk once more. He was working away on a botanical paper. I could get nothing further out of him. So far as he was concerned the subject of the murders was temporarily suspended. I returned to my fiendish statistics.

It must have been about half-past twelve when the telephone jangled harshly. The old man got heavily to his feet and stumped over to the table where it stood. He lifted the receiver slowly, a treatment which it rarely received from him. He looked at the receiver for a moment before he placed it to his face.

"Uhhuh," he said, "I thought so . . . ye're wrong. I'll come along now an' see ye about it. I just got one or two things to do first. All right. I tell ye ye are quite wrong. That's all I can say at the moment."

Still treating the telephone delicately as if it had been a new seedling, he laid it down and turned his heavy face towards me.

"Ye were right, Max," he said slowly, "the Bishop's gone an' arrested Henry Gray."

"What'll you do about your money?" I asked, remembering the cheque he had given Gray the afternoon we first met. I thought it was typical of the old man to behave like that. He is astonishingly generous. I know, as I've had some of it.

"Oh," he dismissed it airily, "that don't matter. They won't hang Gray. He'll be out before ye can say Jack Robinson. Uhhuh."

The look of unhappiness again came into his face. He mumbled to himself.

"The trouble is," he growled, "that I got to act now. Ye'll perhaps bear it in mind that I didn't want to act in this case. I wanted to let sleepin' things lie quiet. Still, I got to get Gray off. I can't let them try him for a murder he didn't commit. No. I mightn't be able to get him off. There's only one way out."

Again he sighed heavily. He went slowly through to his bedroom. I could hear him tossing clothes about and opening drawers as he dressed. It did not take him long. He reappeared in the big room and went and drew himself a quart of beer which he downed at one gulp.

In the hall he knocked on the door beyond which Mrs. Farley and her husband live.

"I'm sorry, Mrs. Farley," he said politely, "I'm afraid I won't be in to lunch. I got to go out an' I'm takin' Mr. Boyle wi' me."

She looked at him fondly. Mrs. Farley adores the old man, in spite of the fact that she likes things to be in apple-pie order.

"Oh Professor Stubbs," she said, "there you go again. You won't forget to eat, will you?"

Gravely the old man assured her that he would try to remember to eat. I had no hopes. My stomach felt the pangs of hunger that would grow greater as the afternoon went on. I knew we would go lunchless.

The Professor, for once, did not hurry, as he drove the Bentley. He sounded his horn on corners and allowed himself to be overtaken and passed by tradesmen's vans. I began to worry about him. I wondered if he was feeling well. This was not the sort of behaviour which I was used to from him. I believe I would rather have been terrified by the recklessness of his driving than worried by the lack of it. I realised that, although we may fight like Bedlington terriers, I am very fond of the Professor. After all, he gave me a start when I was in a pretty average hole, and I owed him something for that. It mayn't be a quiet life living with him, but there are many lives which would be a damn sight worse. This uncanny care in driving worried me.

I needn't have been so concerned about him. He stormed into the Yard like a panzer division going into action. He burst open the Chief Inspector's door before the escorting constable had time to announce him.

The Chief Inspector, large and bland, sat behind his desk. He looked up as the avalanche that was John Stubbs crashed through his door.

"Oi," the old man sounded and looked furious, "What d'ye mean by goin' round arrestin' people wi'out consultin' me? I could ha' saved ye a lot o' trouble. I'd ha' told ye that Gray didn't murder either Leslie or Baird. I know who done it. Dam' ye."

The Chief Inspector did not seem to be impressed. He looked at the Professor with eyes half-closed.

"Oh, John," he said sleepily, "that's the trouble with you. You always know the answers to all questions. If you're not right first time you try again. It's a matter of permutations and combinations. You are bound to be right some time. By the law of averages, you are bound to be right on your first guess occasionally. When you are you won't believe that things can be that way and so you go away and try and prove everyone else guilty. You won't believe plain evidence."

The old man was hopping mad. He laid into the Chief Inspector.

"Look here," he roared indignantly, "me, I got the scientific mind. Me, I'm a scientist an' I'd ha' ye remember that. I got to see why any single person might ha' committed the crime. I got to try everyone in the position o' villain before I can say which o' them is the most likely. I got to convince meself that I'm not tryin' to make the facts fit the case, parin' pieces off them here mentally an' addin' bits there. I got to know the facts an' I got to work on these facts an' on nothin' else. I got to get things straight in me mind. An' here ye are accusin' me o' vacillatin' like a dam' weather-cock. Ye thunderin' well know ye're wrong."

The Chief Inspector did not give way before this tirade. He smiled at the Professor.

"Come, come, John," he said soothingly, "you must admit that this idea of yours that you approach everything in the scientific manner might appear to the layman, like myself, a matter of pure trial and error, dictated by guess-work."

The old man scowled fiercely. He blew noisily through his moustache. He grunted angrily and lowered himself into a chair. I had already taken a seat. It was as cheap to sit as to stand.

"All right, all right," he was pretty testy, "have it your own way. You got the official mind. Ye won't believe I got anythin' to go on but guess work. All right. You won't believe I got the mechanical mind, an' ye say I drink too much beer. I tell you I got the scientific mind, an' I know that I dehydrate quicker than most people. I proved it by experiment. I like gadgets. I got the mechanical mind.

Me, I got the proper mental equipment for a detective. I'm no dam' civil servant. I see a point an' go an grab it. What do I get?" He looked round us with an expression that said he was the worst treated man in the world. "Do I get thanks? No! Does anyone say how clever I am? No! All they say is that I've tried all the possible answers an' I've found the right one. They say I got luck. I say I got brains. Bah!"

He snorted in the direction of the Bishop.

"Dam' ye, Reggie," his voice had become peevish, "what d'ye want to go arrestin' Gray for anyhow. Young Max here last night worked out a kinda case against him an' I told him he was wrong. I also told him," his voice became pleasantly reminiscent, "that I thought the dam' fool coppers, meanin' you, Reggie, were workin' on the same line. Let's see yer case against Gray."

The case, when we came to examine it, was not very much stronger than my case. There were certainly one or two other facts that had been added to it. Gray had, that morning, drawn nearly six hundred pounds from his bank. He had insisted upon having it in one pound notes. There was also the record of three payments, on three successive months, of the sum of fifteen pounds to Cecil Baird. A fourth payment would have been due to-day I realised suddenly.

The Professor snorted and grunted as the Chief Inspector unwound his case. The Chief Inspector kept his trump card to the last. This was that he had discovered a witness who had seen Gray leaving Wesley Street, at least ten minutes after he was supposed, by the time-table the Bishop had prepared, to have left it. This witness, a newspaper seller, was positive that it was Gray he had seen. He described him accurately and mentioned the small portfolio under his arm.

The old man slumped further and further into his chair as the Chief Inspector proceeded with his recital. He lit his pipe and re-lit it several times. He was listening carefully. I could see that he was ready to pounce upon any inaccuracy or inconsistency in the Chief Inspector's case. There didn't seem to be one.

I would have believed that Gray was guilty but for one thing. That one thing was that the old man had told me that he was not guilty. I would take the old man's word for a thing like that against anyone in the world. There had been a time when I would have argued with him, but now I knew that when he had made up his mind he was pretty damn likely to be correct. The Chief Inspector placed detail upon detail and brick upon brick. He built up his case fairly and slowly. No one could accuse him of making up his mind in a hurry.

Professor Stubbs fought bitterly over several points in the case against Gray. He said that there was no reason to suppose that Gray was seriously worried by the attentions of Baird. I felt, myself, that Gray had been pretty foolish in not confiding to the old man that he had been paying money to Baird, but I supposed that he had felt that that would have been a matter that was nobody's business except his own. His conscience had worried him about not admitting to know Baird and he had looked around to explain the fact that he knew Baird, and had hit on the drawing, which was probably quite a true story, as a convenient way out, without admitting that he had also been paying in cash.

When the Chief Inspector let his case rest, he looked pretty pleased with himself. I could see that he had reason to look pleased. Though there was no direct tie between Baird and Leslie and Gray at the exact time of the murders, the Chief Inspector had made out a pretty strong circumstantial case against Gray. I wondered how it would stand up in court. The beastly bit of it was that it looked as though it might stand up in court rather well.

The Professor sighed deeply. He looked even more depressed than he had done when he left the house. He scowled at me, without seeing me. He was very worried.

"Look'ee here, Reggie," he said slowly, "will ye take me word for it that young Gray didn't murder Baird an' Leslie, eh? Will ye get him up here an' apologise for yer mistake?'

"You know, John," the Chief Inspector's tone verged on the official, "that I can't do that. I have a perfectly good case against Gray and I cannot release him until I have a better case against someone else. If you provide me with definite evidence that someone else murdered these two men, then I will most certainly apologise to Gray and release him. But, until I can see that anyone else committed the murders I have to hold Gray. I am convinced that Gray is guilty and that is enough for me. You know me, John Stubbs, and you know that I do not move unless I'm fairly sure of myself. When I am sure I move and I know I am right in this case. Gray is guilty."

"All right then," the old man's voice was heavy and tired, "you can have it. I'll prove to you that Gray was innocent. I'll shew you who was the murderer. I didn't want to have to do that for I ha' me own ideas about the murder an' I feel that it was pretty largely accidental.

To shew you who was guilty we got to go callin'. No, no, Reggie," as the Chief Inspector reached toward the phone, "ye may be frightened o' me drivin', but ye'll ha' to stomach yer fright. Either ye come wi' me or not at all. I know the answer to this case, an' I'll shew it to ye me own way. Come on now."

I had been right when I had guessed that we would not have any lunch. The old man lumbered straight out and climbed into the Bentley. We climbed up beside him.

Chapter 20

The Puzzle Clears

LIKE AN Indian god on the chariot of Juggernaut, the old man sat in the driving seat of the Bentley. He turned round to us and his face was as heavy as lead. I could see that there were tired lines around his eyes and, behind his moustache, at the corners of his mouth.

"Ye haven't announced yer arrest, ha' ye?" he glowered at the Chief Inspector. "If ye ain't, ye'll save yourself some trouble when ye come to sortin' thin's out. I got a few questions I want to ask to get things straight. We're callin' on Miss Wright."

The drive to Streatham was almost terrifying in its sedateness. I think that, like myself, the Bishop was worried by this. Although they spar like a couple of fighting cocks, Professor Stubbs and the Chief Inspector are really inseparable. One without the other is like an accumulator with one of the poles missing.

As we drew up before Miss Wright's house we saw a tall well-built man coming away from it. He was carrying a small bag and there was that indefinable something about him that said that he was a doctor and not a solicitor. He entered a large car and drove off, with hardly a glance at us.

Miss Wright kept us waiting for a few moments before she opened the door. When she did she was as charming as ever and full of apologies.

"I'm so sorry," she said, "to have had to keep you waiting like this, but I've had a visit from my doctor, and," she flushed slightly, "I had to make myself presentable again. Do come in."

She led the way to the drawing-room, her chatelaine jangling as she walked ahead of us. Once we were all seated she looked at the clock on the mantelpiece.

"I'm afraid it's a little early for tea, isn't it," she said brightly, "but would you like to have some coffee?"

"That 'ud be very civil o' ye, ma'am," the old man replied. She bustled off, to reappear in a few minutes with a tray. On this was perched an immense brass coffee percolator, heated with a little spirit lamp. She placed this on the table and sat down. She looked round us.

"Now what can I do for you?" she asked, "I hope you haven't come to ask me a lot more questions. I think I have told you all I know."

"I'm sorry, ma'am," the old man was heavily apologetic, "that's just what I've got to do. Ye see, the police have arrested young Gray for murderin' yer uncle an' Cecil Baird."

At that moment the coffee bubbled up in the percolator and Miss Wright busied herself with pouring out cups for us. She sat straight up in her chair. She looked very frail in the half light of her drawing-room, filtering through the heavy lace curtains. She looked at the Professor with a surprised air.

"But surely, Professor Stubbs," she said precisely, "they can't do that. You see he didn't do the murders."

"I know that, ma'am," the Professor took a sip of his coffee, "an' that's why I came to ye for help. Ye see, I'd ha' lain low an' held me tongue, but the case that the Chief Inspector here has made is very strong, very strong indeed, an' the only way out of it is for you to help me find the real murderer."

Miss Wright looked slightly puzzled. I noticed that she had not tasted her cup of coffee. It sat steaming beside her on a little mahogany table. Her thin hands played with the silver chains of her chatelaine. She smiled at the Professor.

"But surely they can't hang that nice young man—he has such a charming wife—for a murder which he didn't do?"

The old man bowed his head heavily. The mop of grey hair fell down over his forehead and he swept it back with a thrust of his hand.

"I'm afraid, ma'am," his voice was gentle and deep, "that that might happen. There ha' been miscarriages o' justice before in this country. They ain't common but they ha' happened. So ye see why I got to find who did the killin'. I know why it was done an' all that, an' I think I can say I sympathise."

Miss Wright nodded her head with a quick bird-like gesture.

"You know, Chief Inspector," she said simply, "you must let that young man go. He didn't kill anyone. You see I killed them."

The Chief Inspector sat up as if someone had stuck a pin into him. He looked at Miss Wright incredulously. She sat with her hands folded in her lap. Only the finger fiddling with the chain of her chatelaine shewed her nervousness.

"You know what you're saying, ma'am?" the Bishop demanded.

She nodded her head as she answered slowly, "Yes, Chief Inspector, I know what I'm saying."

"In that case," the Chief Inspector was official, "it is my duty to warn you that anything you say may be produced in evidence."

He would have gone on, but Miss Wright held up her hand and he became silent.

"I know what I'm saying," she repeated slowly, "I'm saying that I killed my uncle and that horrible man Baird. It was not until afterwards that I realised quite what I had done."

Her voice quavered slightly and the old man leaned forward,

"Take it easy, ma'am," he said seriously, "take it easy. Don't ride yerself too hard."

Miss Wright pulled herself if anything more upright in her chair.

"Thank you Professor," she smiled at him. "I am an old lady and I have nothing to fear. Less than nothing. As I told you the doctor has just been here to see me. I have a cancer and I cannot live very long. Dr. Robertson didn't want to tell me, but I have believed all my life in facing the facts. I want to face them now. I killed Uncle Allan and Mr. Baird."

The Chief Inspector was sitting on the edge of his chair like a large Persian cat watching a bird it intends to catch. The old man turned his head towards him and he relaxed a little.

"It is quite simple," Miss Wright went on, and her voice was as normal as the voice in which she would have offered me tea, "I went round to call on my uncle. I had bought him a present. A new gas-ring. As I went into the shop I saw my uncle bending over the body of Mr. Baird and I jumped to the conclusion that he had killed him. As soon as this thought came into my mind I could see that my uncle would be arrested and tried for murder. I do not think I could have stood that. All the notoriety would have been too distressing for an old lady like myself."

She noticed that the Professor had finished his coffee. She held out her hand for his cup. He passed it obediently. She poured the coffee with as steady a hand as if nothing was happening. She passed it back to the Professor with a smile.

"Where was I?" she said, "Oh yes. I do not think that I could have borne to see my uncle tried for murder. Murder is a very grave sin. On the spur of the moment I lifted my umbrella and I hit him on the back of the head with it. He fell over. I did not know what I should do. I was alone in the shop with a dead man and with my uncle in an insensible condition. I looked out of the shop door. There was no one in Wesley Street. If there had been I think I would have called for help. But things were not to be that way. On the floor beside my uncle was the envelope of papers which I gave to you, Professor. I picked them up and I realised what a bad man Mr. Baird had been. I put them in my hand-bag and I went out of the door. I bolted it behind me. I looked in my bag and I found two shillings which I placed in the gas-meter. Then I came home. It was not until I was home that I realised what I had done. You see all along I thought that Mr. Baird was dead and that my uncle had murdered him. I had to see what was happening so I left the house. You know the rest."

The Chief Inspector beside me was beginning to rise to his feet. Professor Stubbs put a hand on his knee and pushed him back into his chair.

"I knew that, ma'am," the old man was almost as quiet as Miss Wright. "But ye see, I thought ye'd probably be sufferin' enough, an' unless the police had arrested someone else I kinda intended to hold me peace. Ye, in a moment o' shall we call it madness, set yourself up as a judge o' right an' wrong. I wouldn't do that for meself. I thought that if nothin' happened I would let the dead bury their dead an' all the rest o' it. I hope ye'll understand, ma'am, that it was the unfortunate chain o' circumstances which forced me into this."

"I understand, Professor," she smiled at him primly. She seemed very tired. I put it down to the strain of the afternoon and the fact that she was mortally ill. "I must thank you for all your kindness to an old lady who was nothing to you. I must thank you for your thoughtfulness in coming to me yourself and in not sending round a policeman to arrest me. I can still retain some of the decencies of life in this way."

She looked around her drawing-room with pleasure. The potted palms nodded their leaves slowly in the half-light. The dark-green marble clock ticked gently away on the mantelpiece and Perseus still rescued Andromeda. The pictures hung unmoved upon the walls. Miss Wright looked at her room with a kind of fondling delight. I thought she was thinking how permanent these things were, how they would remain after she had gone, after we had taken her away and after the fierce cancer had finally gnawed out her vitals. I felt inexpressibly sad. She had been kind to us. She was a charming and intelligent old lady.

I knew now why the Professor had been so gloomy all day. He had seen the necessity for this interview looming ever larger, and he had not wished it to take place.

"It was not as though I was not prepared for this," Miss Wright brought her thoughts back from her room to its occupants. "I knew that you realised the truth, Professor Stubbs, as soon as you had finished looking through the papers I gave you the other afternoon. I did not know how you had discovered it, but I knew that you knew. It was foolish of me to keep these papers and foolish of me to give them to you. But I could not resist the temptation to produce the evidence of Mr. Baird's badness. I felt that by doing so I was to some extent excusing myself for my action. I had killed a man, certainly, my uncle who, whatever he did, was not a bad man, but in killing Mr. Baird with him I considered that I had committed no crime. Mr. Baird as I now know was a man who caused very much unhappiness. If his death has brought happiness to anyone then I am content."

Her voice was growing more tired. I could see that the strain was telling upon her. She looked round the room again, appraising the bamboo whatnots and the linen and lace antimacassars. The needles of the juniper beside the door shivered gently in a slight draught.

The Chief Inspector could no longer be restrained. He pushed away the Professor's hand. He rose slowly to his feet.

"Miss Wright," his official voice was gentle and I noticed that he gave her her title and did not address her by her Christian names, "I am afraid that what you have told me leaves me no option. I shall have to take you into custody on the charge of having murdered Allan Leslie and Cecil Baird."

She held up one hand. I noticed how thin and transparent it was. It was like a saint's hand carved out of alabaster, translucent and pale. The blood vessels were like the veining of marble.

"I understand, Chief Inspector," she spoke slowly and with some apparent difficulty, "You have your duty to do. I hope that now you know the truth you will give orders to release that unfortunate young man and will let him return to his wife. If you wish to use the telephone you will find it in the hall."

I don't know what it was about Miss Wright. I think it was her attitude that this was her house and that she was used to being obeyed in it. The Chief Inspector went as meekly as a schoolboy to the door. He did not shut it behind him. I could see that as he dialled he was watching Miss Wright out of the corner of his eye. He gave orders for the release of Henry Gray and other orders dealing with the reception of Miss Wright.

While he was speaking I also was watching Miss Wright. The strain had finally told on her. She lay back in her chair with her eyes half closed. Curiously enough there was a half smile at the corners of her mouth.

The Professor sat slumped directly opposite her. He did not seem to be aware of what was happening around him. His forehead was creased. The unhappiness had died from his face. He knew where he was. I had noticed that as soon as Miss Wright had mentioned the fact that she was dying of cancer, the gloomy cloud which had been sitting on the old man's shoulders all morning had begun to lift. The fact that he was no longer as worried as he had been had not, however, restored his usual boisterousness. He had been as gentle as I have ever seen him. Usually he deals with human beings as if they were all as tough as he is, reserving his tenderness for plants. All I can say is that he treated Miss Wright as if she had been an especially rare plant. Those who know the old man will know how much I mean by this.

The telephone in the hall tinkled. The Chief Inspector came slowly back into the room. He came to a pause before Miss Wright. She opened her eyes with some difficulty. It seemed to me that she had almost fallen asleep.

"Miss Wright," he was polite and unofficial now. I could see he was not really keen on his job, "I have asked for a woman detective to help you pack some things. If, as I gather, you are ill, you will be sent to hospital. I hope that I can make things as easy as possible for you."

She smiled at him.

"I am an old woman," she said irrelevantly, "and I have no life to look forward to. I have taken life and it is right that my life should be forfeit in return. I always thought an eye for an eye and a tooth for a tooth a cruel law, but perhaps it is a just one. I killed in a fit of what the Professor is kind enough to describe as madness, and I hope that I will be forgiven for that.".

Her voice was terribly weary. She looked round her room once more. Her eyes paused on all the things that she most valued. She smiled gently to herself.

"I hope also, Chief Inspector," she said slowly and painfully, "that I will be forgiven for what I have done. You see I am an old woman and have reached an age where it seems more fitting that things should move slowly and with a certain decorum. When the doctor left and I saw that you were with the Professor and Mr. Boyle I knew what you had come for. I have pain sometimes," she seemed to be wandering from the subject, "and Dr. Robertson is kind to me. He gives me pills to take away the pain. I have not taken any since the murders. I have been saving them up. This afternoon Dr. Robertson left me another box. He knew me and he trusts me not to take more than I am ordered to take so he gives me a great many in each box. It saves me running to the chemist. When I looked out of the window and I saw you waiting, I knew that it was time and so I took all the pills I had."

The Chief Inspector opened his mouth, but the Professor kicked him on the shins.

"It is so easy," Miss Wright went on, "to go this way, and so much more comfortable. I always thought I would like to die surrounded by my things. I would not like to die in a hospital bed far away from everything I have treasured."

Her voice was slow and gentle. She took one last look round the room and smiled. She closed her eyes.

"Thank you all for being so charming," she said and her head lolled over. She was asleep.

Chapter 21

Mopping Up

I WAS sitting with Professor Stubbs in his room. We were trying to organise his notes so that he could write another chapter of his *History of Botany* from them.

I heard the chugging of a taxi coming up the hill, and the noise of gears being changed. It was an extraordinarily still night. The car stopped at our house and then went off. The door bell rang.

Mrs. Farley shewed the Chief Inspector into the room. We looked up at him expectantly.

"Yes," he nodded slowly, "She had her way. She died among her own possessions. The police surgeon refused to try a stomach-pump on her. He said she was so far gone with cancer that it was a wonder she'd lived so long. She must have been a woman of some spirit. He said that if we tried to save her we would only cause unnecessary suffering and that we had no chance of succeeding."

The old man turned his head. He had lumbered over to the beer barrel in the corner and was filling two tankards. He had already placed a bottle of brandy and a glass ready for the Chief Inspector.

"Ye know, Reggie," he said and his face was untroubled for the first time that day, "I'm glad she went so easy. She was a nice old thing an' as I told ye, the whole murder case was a strin' o' unfortunate accidents, an' yet everythin' was tied up together."

He placed the Chief Inspector in his chair and lowered himself heavily into his own.

"Ye see," his voice was apologetic, "I kinda thought that she'd find some way out. I could see she'd found it when she came into room an' I grew more certain as time went on. Ye see I was sittin' opposite her an' I could see her eyes, an' I was watchin' the pupils grow."

"Well," the Chief Inspector sounded justly annoyed, "why didn't you tell me ? The police surgeon said that if we'd got her immediately after she had taken the things there'd have been a chance of saving her."

"Uhhuh," the old man was brusque, "of savin' her, of savin' her for what? For a trial which was a foregone conclusion wi' a sentence which ye'd never ha' carried out. No, no, Reggie, it was easier the way it was, an' I'm glad o' it. I liked the old girl. She treated me wi' a becomin' seriousness an' she went out o' her way to be nice to young Max here."

The Chief Inspector swirled the brandy in the bubble-glass cradled in his hands.

"All right, John," he said, "have it your own way. From what the police surgeon says it seems improbable that she'd have lived to stand her trial. She might have died at any moment. But what I'd like to know is what you on to her?"

The Professor drained his quart tankard and stumped over to the barrel to refill it. He glowered at the Chief Inspector over the tops of his steel-rimmed glasses which, as usual, had slipped down to the end of his blunt nose.

"It was very simple," he said deeply, "for there was one object which put me on to her. It was nothin' more or less than an umbrella. If ye'll remember she wasn't carryin' one when she came into the shop on the afternoon o' the murder, an' yet there had bin one or two drizzlin' showers durin' the course o' the afternoon. I wouldn't ha' thought anythin' more about this, I'd just ha' assumed that she was one o' those old ladies who don't like carryin' umbrellas. But then when we were interviewin' Gray he mentioned that she carried a brolly wi' an immense knobbly head, so I began to wonder why she should carry a brolly one day an' not the next in this climate. An' then there was the third appearance o' the brolly. I met her outside yer office an' she was carryin' it. Now it was a blinkin' fine day an' there was no possible reason for her to carry it, unless she was one o' those people who always carry an umbrella. I also noticed that the head o' the brolly was unnaturally bright."

He scowled at us. The Chief Inspector helped himself to a cigar from a box beside him. He crackled it at his ear and lit it carefully.

"Go on, John," he said, "I don't see where that got you. She might just have left it somewhere that day, when she wasn't carrying it."

"Dammit, man," the old man was forcible, "did Miss Wright strike ye as the sort o' person who'd go around sheddin' bits o' her property, eh? If she did ye're a bigger fool than I'd ha' taken ye for. No, no. If she carried a brolly on a day it didn't look as though it would rain, she'd most certainly ha' taken it out on an afternoon when it did rain. So ye see, I got that far, an' then it occurred to me that maybe the reason the brolly wasn't wi' her when we first met her was that it was broken, an' that shiny head had looked too new to be passed over. So I asked ye for a little help an' wi'in an hour I found it had bin mended for her in that shop in New Oxford Street—ye know the place—wi' a window full o' walkin' sticks an' sword sticks and ridin' crops. The man could remember her perfectly plainly. She'd brought it in, on the afternoon o' the murder mind ye—an' said she'd dropped it. The man in the shop said it had certainly had a pretty hard crack. She was so insistent on havin' it repaired promptly that they did their best to expedite the job, particularly as the umbrella was one they had sold her in the first place. Then, o' course, it was plain sailin'. Ye'll remember that there was a shillelagh in the back o' Leslie's shop. Yes? Well, no doubt Leslie used that to knock out Baird wi'. As she told ye herself, Miss Wright used her umbrella as a knobkerry. Ye'll notice that every time the thing was mentioned or that we saw it, someone noticed its large head. She didn't, in her confession, tell us she'd broken the umbrella, as that didn't seem to her to be important, but she did confess to usin' it. Ye see I was right."

He crowed like a triumphant cockerel on a dung-hill.

"I got the simple mind I have," he went on, "ye were all trying to fix the murder on this one an' that while I was tryin' to see how the hell ye'd knock out two people by hittin' them on the back o' the heads. I drew Max's attention to this problem an' he tried to slur it over in his case against Gray, just as you did, Reggie. Well it seemed to me, con-siderin' Baird's activities, that the most likely thing to ha' happened was that Leslie had knocked Baird on the head in order to take some papers off him, an' that someone else had knocked Leslie on the head in turn. Once I got the papers I was sure o' it, an' sure o' me case against Miss Wright. Ye see Leslie's name was not among those ticked off on Baird's register, an' yet the damnin' papers were in Leslie's house. The only way they could ha' got there was for them to ha' bin taken by Miss Wright. Considerin' the lack o' the tick, they couldn't ha' bin left there the pre-vious evenin' by Leslie himself. Baird was the kinda feller who'd ha' ticked off each o' his victims as soon as he left 'em."

He moved himself heavily in his chair and re-lit his pipe which had gone out while he was talking.

"Until she got the story straight, ye see, Miss Wright was more or less lookin' upon herself as the instrument o' Divine Providence. Her uncle had killed a man an' she had killed him in turn. She didn't feel bad about it either, for God was busily engaged in killin' her, slowly an' painfully. The triangle o' death was complete. She was clear in her conscience. It was only when she discovered that she had killed not only her uncle but Baird also that she began to take it bad. The shock it must ha' bin to her when she read these papers and thought o' them in connection wi' her uncle's knockin' Baird out must ha' shaken her pretty thoroughly. But she still did not feel impelled to come forward an' make a clean breast o' the whole affair. No, the pain she was feelin' was a direct punishment for havin' dared to take Divine Vengeance into her hands. She said, ye'll remember, that she hadn't taken any o' her pills since the murder. She said she was savin' them up. That was her pride comin' out, she could not confess that she had bin mortifyin' her flesh by refusin' to swallow the pain-killin' drug. What she was doin' was sufferin' her hell for her mistake physically as well as mentally. As she said she liked to face things. Well, she was facin' both the thought o' her terrible mistake, when, for a brief moment, she had seemed to be the direct emissary o' God, an' also the hell o' her cancer eatin' at her, unchecked an' undeadened. She belonged, as she told us, to a generation which had learned to hide its feelin's. Never by a word or gesture did she so much as suggest to either Max or meself the hellish pain she must ha' bin sufferin'. She was as charmin' as could be, an' I'll wager that not even when she was alone did she allow herself to relax."

The Chief Inspector looked enquiringly at the Professor and refilled his brandy-glass.

"All the same," he said, "she didn't strike me as being the kind of religious maniac who would consider that they were doing right by killing the killer. She seemed to me to be far too reasonable a person."

"Humph," the old man snorted, "ye got to consider her as a whole person an' not as parts o' a person. I just gave ye a part of the kinda argument that she might ha' used to herself, to kinda justify herself in the eyes o' her God. Ye've also got to remember that she was a most respectable kinda person. An' that respectable people do the most astonishin' things to preserve their respectability. Thank God," his voice was noisily pious, "I'm not respectable."

He took a long swig at his beer.

"Then you got to consider what it means to have a murderer in the family to that kinda person. Ye see there Miss Wright was, looking in through the door o' her uncle's shop an' she sees her uncle bendin' over what she assumes to be the body o' a man he has just killed. She sees, flashin' before her, the whole thunderin' panoply o' the law. She sees the judge puttin' on his black cap an' she can already hear the neighbours whispering 'There goes Miss Wright, her uncle will be hangin' to-morrow for murderin' a man.' This goes through her mind like lightnin' an' kinda mentally she says to herself, 'Better to ha' murdered uncle than one who's bin hung,' an' so she dots him one an' does her best to muddle the whole affair by shuttin' doors on the outside an' putting money in the gas meter. I got no doubt that once she'd slogged her uncle on the head she was as cool as if she'd been layin' a tray for tea at home. Everythin' would be done in correct order an' then she'd steam out o' the shop an' away towards the Tottenham Court Road Underground station. On the way there she notices that she's cracked the handle o' her brolly and kinda says to herself 'Dam' uncle for havin' such a blinkin' hard head, I'll need to get it mended.' So she trots along New Oxford Street, leaves the brolly wi' instructions that it's to be repaired as soon as possible, goes down the underground an' so home, to a nice cup o' *Earl Grey* tea. Once she gets home, however, she starts wonderin' about whether she's done the right thing. This was the only bit o' weakness she shewed, so she puts on her things a' sallies forth again. She'll ha' missed the presence o' her brolly as she went, but that wouldn't keep her from goin' out. By the time she got back to Wesley Street, she's managed to separate Miss Wright walkin' along the street from Miss Wright who's just bin the personification o' Justice. She acts perfectly natural when she finds out what's happened, an' why shouldn't she? She's genuinely sorry that her uncle's bin murdered. He was a short-tempered man, but he gave her a home where she could have her own things. However appallin' they may appear to our taste, she was fond o' 'em."

The Chief Inspector looked along his cigar like a man sighting along a rifle barrel.

"In fact, John," he said resignedly, "You blundered into the solution by taking the most unlikely person and the most unlikely motive and tying them together. My God, how typical of you."

The Professor snorted angrily. I feared for a moment that he was about to hurl his tankard at the bland face of the Bishop.

"Indeed I did not," he said indignantly, "I tried all yer suspects an' I found them wantin'. I didn't want to believe that Miss Wright was the criminal. The thin' was that once I'd come round to thinkin' about her brolly I had to admit to meself that no one else could ha' done the murder an' so I started tryin' to think up a set o' circumstances which 'ud fit the crime. I worked it out pretty much as we know it now. Ye see, I had some hints about the character o' Allan Leslie from various witnesses in the case, an' they made it clear that, old man though he was, he wasn't the sort who'd put put up wi' too much. He might pay Baird a sum amountin' to ten per cent o' the profits on his dealings in stolen books, but he would probably boggle at the idea o' paying out somewhere in the region of several thousand pounds. 'Oh yes, Baird' he says gentle like, 'I'll have the money ready for ye. Just ye bring along the papers you got concernin' me an' we'll do a fair swap.' Sorta will ye walk into me parlour said the spider business. Well Baird thinks he got nothin' to fear from an old man like Leslie an' along he walks. Leslie clocks him one on the back o' the neck an' Baird passes out. Leslie takes the papers from him an' destroys 'em. Baird wakes up feelin' as though he'd bin out on a thunderin' bat and there's Leslie smiling at him, perhaps offerin' him back his empty envelope, sayin', 'Thank'ee kindly Mr. Baird I destroyed the papers an' what are ye goin' to do about it?' Leslie 'ud ha' bin sittin as pretty as a bird on a fence, for there was nothin' Baird could ha' done about it. Baird 'ud just ha' to go off home nursin' his sore head an' the thought that he'd bin beaten. That was the way it was meant to work out. That it didn't work out that way was just pure dam' bad luck. The shockin' cussedness of luck. If Miss Wright had chosen to call along to see her uncle half an hour later, carryin' her offer o' a new gas-ring, she'd probably ha' bin surprised by the affability o' her reception. Her uncle was sittin' on top o' the world. There was nothin' that could go wrong wi' his scheme. That's the hell o't."

He swigged down some more beer and looked round at us fiercely, as if to say that we must agree with him or he'd know the reason why. I had only one question to ask him.

"Why," I said, "were you so worried about the case? After all, Miss Wright had meant to murder her uncle and so she was strictly a murderer. I'll admit that she was very nice and kind to me, but a lot of murderers have been very nice and kind. Why were you so upset this morning?"

"Yes," the Chief Inspector chipped in, "I've seen you in a lot of cases, John, and you always seem to treat murder as a sort of high-class and rather more exciting poker. It isn't like you to take the side of the killer. Why did you do it?"

"Um," the old man looked round the room as if afraid that someone else might be listening, "Um. I'll tell ye a secret. Trouble wi' me is I had a respectable upbringin' an' I feel for those who ain't bin able to break away from it. Ye see, a respectable upbringin' is the greatest incentive to crime ye can have—if ye want to remain respectable. I'm duly grateful for the fact that I learned its dangers early. Poor Miss Wright kept on to the end imaginin' that it was the only way o' life. Come on, Max, have another pint, an' you Reggie, fill yer glass."

The End

The End

About the Author

RUTHVEN CAMPBELL TODD (1914–1978) was a Scottish-born poet, scholar, art critic, and fantasy novelist who wrote a series of detective novels under the name R. T. Campbell.